LONE WOLF

THE HYBRID WOLF SERIES: PREQUEL

CIARA DELAHUNT

DUBHLUNA
PUBLISHING

Lone Wolf
The Hybrid Wolf Series: Prequel
© 2023 by Ciara Delahunt

Cover art by Anna Spies of Atra Luna Graphik Design

Contact information:
www.ciaradelahunt.com
ciara@ciaradelahunt.com

ISBN: 978-1-7391785-2-9
First Edition: September 2023

CHARACTERS

FAOLCHÚNNA PACK*
Tom Whelan – *surname pronounced 'wee-lan'*
Luke Whelan
Fiachra Whelan
Damien McKenna – pronounced *'day-me-en'*
Nick McKenna
~~Patrick McKenna~~
~~Luke McKenna~~
Mary McKenna
Cormac McKenna
Darren Donohoe
Shane Donohoe
Liz
Aoife – *pronounced 'eef-a'*

** Werewolves unless otherwise indicated.*

OTHER
Baz (*demon*)
Bríana (*human*) - *pronounced 'bree-ana'*
Gráinne (*human*) - *pronounced 'grawn-yah'*
Helena (*human*)
Lars (*vampire*)
Larissa (*witch*) – *pronounced 'la-ris-ah'*
~~Laura Whelan~~ (*werewolf*)
Niamh (*witch*) - *pronounced 'neeve'*
Orfeo (*gargoyle*)

BEFORE YOU READ

I write paranormal romance and as such, my books are aimed at adults. *The Hybrid Wolf Series* includes themes of an adult nature, and violent scenes typical of the paranormal romance and fantasy genres. This book contains certain subjects that some readers may be sensitive to.

Please stay safe and visit my website to check the content warnings for my books before reading:

www.ciaradelahunt.com/content-warnings

IRISH LESSON

Class is in session. By the end of this series, you're going to be fluent in Irish slang.

***Mam* is not a typo!** We don't say mom over here.

I know our names have too many vowels, but revert to this when you get stuck and enjoy the ride.

- **Boreen:** a narrow lane in the countryside
- **Cert:** certificate
- **Chips:** fries (we call chips 'crisps' here)
- **College/university:** interchangeable
- **Craic:** fun/entertaining
- **Faolchúnna:** wolves
- **Flash drive:** USB stick
- **"For fuck's sake!":** exclamation of frustration, similar to 'What the hell?'
- **Fresher:** student in their first year at college in Ireland *(approx. 18 years old)*
- **Garda:** police officer *(Bán Garda is a female police officer)*
- **Gardaí:** police plural
- **Garda station:** police station
- **In the nip:** in the nude
- **Keeping sketch:** view the area for approaching authority
- **Lie in:** to stay in bed later than usual in the morning
- **Lift:** elevator

- **Lose the plot:** lost their mind, to no longer be able to act normally or understand what is happening
- **Luas:** name of the tram service in Dublin
- **Mam:** mom/mother *(the Irish don't use mom)*
- **Path/footpath:** sidewalk
- **Piss:** to pee
- **Puke:** vomit
- **Punter:** your average paying customer
- **Runners:** trainers (shoes)
- **Snug:** a small room or area in a pub where only a few people can sit
- **Strop:** a bad mood
- **Tracksuit bottoms:** joggers
- **Twig:** to suddenly realise something
- **Wing mirror:** side-view mirror on a car
- **"You're taking the piss":** you're pushing it or you better be joking

It's highly possible I've missed something here. If you're ever confused, check my reader groups, or drop me a message on social media!

To the readers who had to lose loved ones to stand up for their beliefs. I see you.

CHAPTER 1

I never expected to get the call—the one telling me our alpha was dead. I remember freezing with the phone against my ear until small hands tugging at my leg brought me back to reality. Staring at my son, his amber eyes filled with innocence matching those of his mother. There was no question in my mind; it was time for us to come home.

Seeing my alpha laid out on top of a pyre was surreal. It felt like I was in some walking nightmare. Luke had been a great alpha—one of the best. I'd always aspired to be like him. His wife was laid out beside him, holding her husband's hand. The story was that he and his wife had died in a car crash. But werewolves healed faster than humans, so I couldn't wrap my head around how a car accident would have killed both of them. Apart from some scratches, they looked like they were sleeping. It wasn't right.

"Come now, Tom," my father walked up behind me, placing a heavy hand on my shoulder. "The ceremony is about to start. Where's little Luke?"

Hello father, how are you? It's so lovely to see you.

But that wasn't how we did things.

I shook my head, rubbing my eyes as if it might make everything go away. "He's at the manor with the rest of the kids, one of the Murphy girls is watching him."

"He should be here, he's old enough."

"Luke is a *toddler*, being surrounded by death is no place for a child," I hissed, doing my best not to cause a scene.

Of course, our first conversation since I got home would be an argument.

Before my father could retort, a young man dressed as his double walked up to us. Damien was like a half-brother, my father had practically raised him and his younger brother Nick. We were two halves mashed into one dysfunctional family. Damien's dad, Patrick, had been my father's best friend. When he passed away, my father took the kids under his wing. I lost my mother the same day. I was only twelve, and she never even got to see my first change.

Damien leaned in to whisper in my father's ear. "Fiachra, it's time."

My father scowled but decided to drop the issue.

We silently fell into place beside the rest of our pack, forming one large circle with the alpha at the centre, standing shoulder to shoulder, each of us wearing the same sombre expression. The pyre stood tall in the centre of the clearing surrounded by trees stretching up as if they were reaching for the stars. The glow of the full moon lit up the clearing, aided by the light of four small fires burning several feet from each corner of the pyre. The heat of the flames cut through the cold winter's night.

On the opposite side of my father, Damien stood beside Nick and his mother. His every movement down to his clasped hands mirrored my father's.

Despite catching the earliest flight from London I could get at such short notice, I had only landed in Dublin late in the evening, which meant I didn't get the chance to talk to anyone before the funeral. I'd just enough time to sort someone to mind Luke and get into a suit. Arriving with the bare essentials, I felt like a child running home to Daddy saying they couldn't hack it, which wasn't too far from the truth. Everyone who caught my eye gave me a nod or even a smile. The few I did get to talk to had welcomed me back with a pat on the shoulder or a hug. Every friendly greeting assured me I had made the right decision coming home.

Further along to my right stood the two children the alpha had left behind. His son Cormac, next in line to be alpha, was barely nineteen. He stood staring resolutely at the ground, his shoulders sagging under an invisible weight. His older sister Mary held his hand, her knuckles almost white, her eyes never leaving her parents.

I swallowed and looked away, my chest tightening. It was all too familiar. Every time I looked at the pyre, I saw my wife, and an old wound reopened.

Once everyone was in position, my father stepped forwards, his head bowed as he walked into the centre of our pack circle, stopping at the base of the pyre. He whispered something, his words so quiet I couldn't pick them up clearly even with my heightened sense of hearing. When he turned to face the congregation, tears glistened in his eyes and he looked haggard, unlike his usual polished appearance.

Damien and I shifted to close the gap, and I gave him an awkward mix of a handshake and a hug before turning my attention back to my father, who cleared his throat.

I could hear the river flowing nearby as the crowd fell silent.

"We are gathered here today to mourn a catastrophic loss," he began, his voice crisp and clear. "A few days ago, we lost two dear members of our pack to a car accident, something most of us can barely fathom. We lost our alpha."

He paused and a choked sob broke the silence.

"Together, as a pack, we are here tonight to pay our respects and mourn one of the greatest alphas to lead the Faolchúnna pack in centuries."

A soft murmur of agreement travelled through the pack, but my father's scripted lines couldn't hold my attention. I cast a quick glance at Cormac. He was an empty shell of himself. Mary was the only thing holding him up. Silent tears streamed down her face, but her jaw was set, and she held herself with so much strength and decorum, I couldn't help but admire her.

"This is a dark time for all of us, especially those family members left behind. Luke was taken too soon, and a good mother was taken with him. It is a tragedy we will never forget."

A woman began weeping on the other side of the pyre but my view of them was blocked.

"However, we must remember that in darkness there is light, and we cannot forget all the wonderful things Luke and Marion have done when they were alive. Luke led this pack for over thirty years, following in his father's footsteps to help us move along with the times and flourish. He was the one who set up our legal firm, giving us jobs and a purpose that fit in with today's society. He always wanted us to walk alongside the modern world. He and Marion had two wonderful children who are a testament to their good values." My father swallowed, and for the first time in my life his imperturbable mask looked like it might crack. "It's a great travesty that Luke should be taken so early, especially when his brother Patrick was taken from us too."

While I struggled to stomach my father's speech, I caught sight of Damien from the corner of my eye. He was hanging on my father's every word.

"I remember when I first became a doctor, I had been away at college for years and that was fine. Hospital placement was a piece of cake. But when one of our own was injured in a street fight with a rival pack, I froze." My father's speech quickly became a monologue.

Of course, he has to make it about him.

I rolled my eyes at his arrogance. I'd heard all the stories and this one hadn't been in the repertoire—not this version anyway. He was retelling an old one, replacing Patrick with Luke to make it fit because he didn't have a true good word to say about the alpha who had always risen above it and treated my father with a respect he didn't deserve.

My father's inability to return that respect even after our alpha had passed shouldn't have surprised me.

"Treating strangers was nothing like treating one of your own, a fellow wolf. But Luke was there, he talked me around and gave me the courage to save that wolf's life. That's what Luke did, he led his pack."

Moving to stand beside one of the fires with his unlit torch raised, my father nodded in a silent signal. Two men stepped forwards with torches in hand, taking up similar positions to form a diamond. Only the fire at the foot of the pyre was left untouched. Beside me, Mary was whispering in Cormac's ear, one hand squeezing his arm and the other placed on his back, gently nudging her brother forwards. He clutched his torch tightly to his chest, his eyes darting from his parents to the fire and then back again. He was shaking so much I thought he might drop the torch altogether.

"Luke and Marion McKenna will always be valued members of our pack." My father's voice boomed as he reached forwards and lit his torch, the flames casting shadows across his face. "They will forever be in our hearts. May they run free for eternity and the full moon guide them always."

Soft murmurs rose as the pack repeated the response.

When Cormac couldn't do it alone, Mary stepped forwards and pried the torch from his hand, wrapping an arm around her brother as they walked in unison towards the fire closest to their parents' feet. She lit the torch, flames dancing in the gentle breeze as they took stilted steps until she reached the base of the pyre.

My gaze met Damien's and for a fleeting moment, and I could swear he looked bored. Seconds later, he had schooled his expression. I was about to pull him up on it but movement by the pyre caught my eye.

Mary took a deep breath, a visible shudder racking her body as she placed the torch in the pyre. The fire caught on to the structure immediately and beginning to expand. As the others added their torches too, flames engulfed the wooden structure.

When she looked up, her eyes shined with tears reflecting the fire burning bright. "May you run forever under the freedom of the moon," she whispered, her voice cracking at the last words. "I love you mam, dad. I promise we'll look after each other."

They stepped back and re-joined the circle, Mary keeping a tight grip on her brother the whole time, murmuring quiet words of promise and comfort though her own composure was slipping. Cormac's haunted gaze remained locked on the fire engulfing the pyre. Losing your parents was hard enough, but having the weight of being alpha on his shoulders at such a young age was too much.

We don't always get to choose our path in life, sometimes the role of alpha chooses the wolf.

CHAPTER 2

After the burial ritual, the pack ran as one under the full moon. As one of the last remaining descendants of the alpha's line, Cormac pulled himself together and led the hunt alongside his sister. It was emotional for all of us, and I was proud of him for managing to get through it. I wasn't sure I could in his position.

It felt good to be home––to be surrounded by the familiar scents of my pack and the forests lining the base of the mountains. But as good as the crisp winter air felt, I ducked out at the first opportunity and loped back to the manor instead. Behind me, wolf calls echoed in the night as the full moon peaked above the treetops, casting an eerie light across our territory. I stepped out of the forest to see a large meadow stretching ahead, a small estate rising beyond it. A handful of houses dotted along a winding path leading up the hill were dwarfed by the manor house sat on top.

It was quiet and peaceful, but the pack would return for the wake soon.

The back door to the manor was left open a crack, just like it always was. I nosed it open and slipped inside, silently padding through the kitchens into the hall, my claws clicking on the old worn floorboards. It looked the same as the day I had left, rich oak floors and high beams crisscrossing the high roof, moonlight filtering in through the large glass windows spaced along the corridors. There had been talk of redesigning, but I was glad they hadn't—I was fond of the rustic feel.

I loped up the stairs and only once I was outside my room did I revert to my human form, quickly slipping inside before anyone could see me. Most of the pack would just traipse through the house butt naked. It was part of being a werewolf, but living in London for a few years had taught me that I didn't need to see the older wolves in that state and the younger wolves didn't need to see it either.

By the time I forced myself out of the sanctuary of the warm shower and dressed, I could hear the murmur of voices beginning downstairs. As I reached the bottom of the staircase, pack members were slowly filtering to and from the kitchens with plates and cutlery. I turned the opposite way towards the other source of noise. I edged the door open to the living area, a giant sitting room of sorts that was usually reserved for more casual gatherings but had now been commandeered by the kids. Too young to hunt or be left at home, it had become an unspoken tradition that they would gather here where the younger children could play, and the teenagers could watch television. Or, if they were smart, sneak a few beers, but maybe that was my misspent youth.

On the couch, Luke's babysitter, Aoife—one of the pack teenagers who hadn't shifted yet—was curled up watching a movie while Luke snored away beside her. She gave me a thumbs up, and I quickly tore myself away, closing the door behind me. I knew that if I woke him, I'd never make it to the wake. I had to show my face. Not going just wasn't worth the aggro.

The hum of conversation grew louder as I returned to the

heart of the manor and walked through a formal dining room into a larger function room, already brimming with pack members gathered in small groups, talking animatedly. While losing a pack member was a huge blow to the pack, we viewed the wake as a celebration of life, not as a time to mourn. I wasn't sure if it was a werewolf thing or us carrying over Irish traditions but hearing happy stories about those we had lost and looking back fondly on memories always brought me some comfort.

"Tom!"

The sound of my name distracted me from eyeing the beer line-up and I spun just in time to see Mary approaching. She wore a long black dress and despite the circumstances still looked like she was holding it together. The only give-away was the mascara smudges under her eyes. She reached to shake my hand awkwardly, but when I pulled her in for a hug, her shoulders sagged ever so slightly.

"It's so good to see you home," she said, her lips curving into a small smile as she stepped back. Pain dulled the sparkle in her eyes, despite her best efforts to cover it up. "How long has it been?"

"Over a year?" I shrugged, guilt knotting my shoulders. "Not since Christmas last year…"

Was it really that long?

"I really should've visited more." Mary dropped her gaze, scuffing the floor with her feet.

"I wasn't much fun to be around."

The usual awkward silence that followed was replaced with a sombre sense of understanding. It had been almost two years since my wife's death and I still wasn't sure what to say. Losing her the same night as Luke came into my life was like losing one love and gaining another. It had been the hardest thing. It was the pity I couldn't handle--the look that people gave when they found out I was a widower. The first year, I'd brought Luke home to meet my side of the family properly at Christmas for a handful of days. It was a painful blur; I had barely spoken a word to anyone. Since then, I'd hid out in London, burying myself in work. The longer I stayed there, the more I withdrew.

"You back for good?" she asked, bringing me back to the present.

I swallowed, catching sight of my father regaling some poor unfortunates with his hero stories. "It was time. The London pack are great but with Laura gone... it just wasn't the same."

She reached out to give my hand a gentle squeeze. "It's the right decision. You need to be with your pack. You're living in the main house?"

"Yep, perks of joining the medical team here," I quipped, forcing a grin.

"It doesn't count when your daddy is the pack doctor." She rolled her eyes, giving my arm a gentle thump.

"It's good for the kid though, and you have your own space, right? I'm sure if you asked to build your own house, the alph—" She stopped mid-sentence, her face paling as reality hit her all over again.

I knew that feeling, the one where you forget for just a split second. It hurts like a bitch.

"The manor isn't so bad," I said quietly, quickly changing the subject. "At least until I get a placement at a local hospital, then maybe I can justify having my own space."

Realisation lit up her face, closely followed by a wave of sadness. "You called him Luke, didn't you?"

It took me a moment to realise she was talking about my son. Heat rose to my cheeks, the name choice felt more poignant now that our alpha was dead.

"Yeah, I—eh, Laura and I wanted him to have a piece of

my pack." I rubbed the back of my neck, swiping a bottle of the nearest beer.

She nodded, the ghost of a smile tugging at her lips at the sentiment. "It's sweet."

I knocked back a mouthful of beer, waiting for the burn that never came. I was going to need something stronger to get through another funeral.

"So, how do you get through one of these?" she asked, gesturing at the crowd.

It felt surreal coming back under these circumstances. Mary had been one of my closest friends growing up. She was like a little sister, but in a way, we felt like strangers talking. It was my fault. The longer I stayed in London, the more we grew apart.

"You pretend that you're okay, listen to a few stories." I moved further along the drinks table, picking up what looked like an expensive bottle of red and pouring a more than generous glass which I handed to my old friend with a sympathetic smile. "And then you knock this back to get through it."

She shot me a reproachful look but took a sip of the wine, exhaling slowly. "It wouldn't be a real wake without a drink, would it?"

If Irish werewolves were good at anything, it was a celebration.

"It's a long day, you need something to keep you going."

Mary nodded, her eyes misting over as she looked out at the crowd and zeroed in on her brother.

Cormac stood across the room, surrounded by two other guys around his age. They didn't do much talking, their main focus knocking back as many beers as they could. Their rising laughter and unstable sway gave away how much drink had already gone to their heads.

"So, what have I missed?"

Mary shrugged, running the tip of her finger around the rim of her glass. "Nothing much, things were pretty normal. Dad was working on the same old stuff, some treaties with the witches, the law firm was doing really well. I was supposed to intern there this summer."

"Supposed to?" My brow furrowed. I remembered her having arguments with her parents years ago. She was the first woman in the pack to go to college and graduated with straight honours. "You can still go."

"I took a year out after the master's degree to give myself a break, but I never thought it would end like this." Mary trailed off, uncertainty seeping into her every word. "I can't leave him now. The pressure of becoming alpha so young is crushing him."

"But you'd only be gone during the day."

"Does he look like he can cope with only seeing me at dinner?" she snapped, her words cutting. Sadness engulfed her soft features at the harshness of her words. "Cormac's a mess. He needs someone to keep an eye on him. That's my job now."

I opened my mouth but when Mary had her mind set, there was no arguing with her. She wasn't entirely wrong.

"I'm here now. If you need my help, just ask," I said quietly.

Her brief smile faltered, and I turned my head to see Damien snaking his way through the crowd towards us. I caught Mary wearing the same wary expression as me.

"What? Don't look at me like that." She snorted, leaning over to whisper in my ear. "I've never liked the guy, and he hasn't changed one bit. He's still that awkward, quiet, creepy little kid—" She cut herself off as Damien stepped within hearing distance, plastering the fakest of smiles on her face. "Hi Damien."

"Hello cousin." He inclined his head politely. "I'm sorry for your loss."

"Thank you." She pursed her lips, slinging her arm around me in a quick hug before stepping away to make her excuses. "I better mingle, talk to you later?"

I nodded, watching her disappear into the throng of people now gathered in the function room. I made a beeline for the patio doors, doing my best not to get drawn into conversation as different pack members smiled and shook my hands to welcome me home.

A cool breeze washed over me as I stepped outside, a blanket of stars stretching across the lawn. Damien fell into step beside me, one hand in his pocket as he strolled along. I sucked in a deep breath and exhaled. Tension with my father had pushed me to move to London, and while it was a lovely place, there was nowhere like home.

Several small fires lit up the gardens, their flames licking the night sky. A group of men huddled around the barbecue, other groups stood laughing and chatting. In the distance, the full moon hung above the dark silhouette of the forest and the mountains.

"It's good to have you back where you belong." Damien finally broke the silence, producing a cigarette from his pocket.

"Thanks, it's kind of nice to be back, though I wish it was under better circumstances."

As he lit the cigarette and popped it in his mouth, I couldn't help noticing the similarity to my father. Just because he was a werewolf and could heal, it didn't change the fact that it was gross. We didn't get nicotine addictions because it wasn't strong enough to have lasting effects, so I could never understand the appeal.

"Damien, what are you doing man?"

He shrugged, taking a drag. "It doesn't do any harm, just takes the edge off."

"What edge?" I asked, my tone coming sharper than I had expected. "You're not under any pressure."

I wasn't sure where he got off talking like he was some world hardened man. He was barely two years my senior.

He snorted. "You've been gone for years remember? I've been helping your dad out a fair bit when I'm not at the office."

"You're just everywhere," I said, resisting the urge to punch him as he flicked the ashes from his cigarette into the flower bed.

When I went off to college, my father had asked me not to become a doctor. It was the only thing we had in common, but he wanted me to get a law degree and join the firm that our alpha had built to honour his brother's legacy. Despite our differences, I had seen him save lives. It was in my blood. When Damien's turn came, he chose to study law and my father couldn't have been prouder.

Damien cocked his head, studying my face with that unnerving steely gaze of his. "You look stressed, Tom. London hasn't been kind to you."

"Losing a wife and raising a kid alone will do that to you," I muttered, doing my best to ignore the heat rising in my body. He hadn't lost his talent for getting under my skin. "Thanks for coming to the funeral by the way."

"I had an important case, otherwise you know I'd have been there," he said flatly, giving me a not so gentle pat on the back. "You're my brother, it killed me to miss it."

"Uh-huh, I'm sure it did *brother.*"

"Look." Damien dropped his cigarette and smudging it into the grass with his heel. "Me and some of the others are going for drinks in town after this, if you fancy joining us?"

Do not punch him.

I opened my mouth, ready to take him down a notch, but I snapped it shut and shook my head in dismay. "Here was me thinking you had grown up a bit. This is a wake, our alpha is *dead*, and you want to go clubbing? Don't you think you should stick around and support your pack? Mary and Cormac just lost their parents."

"It's a few drinks, Tom," he scowled like a petulant child, folding his arms across his chest. "People die all the time."

"Where is your respect? He was your alpha."

Damien shrugged, the corners of his lips twitching. "And now he's not."

CHAPTER 3

Walking up the winding stairs leading to the alpha's suite on the top floor of the house felt strange. It was a living area, so in the days Luke was still alive, I rarely visited him. Most of my visits up there had been to hang out with Mary. The memory of her sneaking me and a few others up to her room for drinks when we were underage and her parents were away on pack business surfaced in my mind, tugging at the corners of my lips. Things were so simple back then.

At the top of the stairs was a small landing with four doors that led to three bedrooms and one living area. Instead of heading for the familiar door on the left with Mary's name carved into it, we stood together in front of the main door. It was old oak, the same as the rest, but had silver trimmings and designs embedded in the wood, depicting the forest leaves, the moon, and a wolf howling into the night.

I looked at Mary, who seemed to be holding her breath, and gave her a gentle nudge.

"I can't do this." She shook her head, dark circles lining her eyes as she wrung her hands and began to back away.

All the strength she had shown at the funeral, the set of

her shoulders, had diminished. I'd never seen her so skittish. She was always brimming with confidence, had a snake-bite tongue and a humour to match.

When Mary had asked me to help her go through her parent's things a few weeks after the funeral, my first instinct was to refuse. I didn't want to risk bringing back bad memories, but I felt like a coward. There she was, carrying on with strength and looking after her brother on top of everything, and here I was feeling sorry for myself. I'd promised myself that moving home was a fresh start, so I needed to stop hiding from the past. My friend needed me.

"It's not going to be easy, but you can do this." I slung an arm around her shoulders to pull her in for a hug. "There will never be a right time."

Mary nodded, chewing her lower lip. "Okay, I'm ready."

She might have well stuck an 'I think' at the end because she seemed as sure about that choice as I did about jumping off a cliff.

I unlocked the door, pushing it wide open before stepping inside. The room had been left completely untouched, one of the alpha's suits still hanging on the wardrobe. The master bed was made, with some books stacked on the beside locker that must have belonged to Mary's mother, along with a football magazine. Perfume and makeup bottles lined the dressing table beneath the mirror with a few pictures, along with a crayon drawing stuck to it. It looked as if nothing had changed.

Mary stood in the doorway, her chest rising and falling erratically.

"It's ok, we'll do this one step at a time," I reassured her, reaching out to coax her into the room.

She pulled her hand away, wrapping her arms around her torso, taking slow stilted steps until she was in the centre of the room. Her eyes filled with tears as she turned in one full circle.

"It's so... normal."

I nodded, dipping out of the room for a moment to bring in the black bags and cleaning products we had readied. "It was the same with Laura."

A flicker of guilt crossed her features. "I shouldn't have asked you to help."

"No," I said firmly, dropping the stuff on the bed. "I want to help. We just need to start, it gets easier then."

From experience, I decided to start with the chest of drawers. Socks were less upsetting than the more personal items. I pulled one drawer out and tipped the contents onto the bed.

"One step at a time." I forced a strained smile as I handed her a black bag to put the clothes for charity in.

Mary set about sorting through the contents of the drawers before we moved on to do the wardrobe. Seeing things like her father's best suit and her mother's wedding dress set her off a few times. Discussion flowed between reminiscing about the old days, crying, and hugs. Bit by bit, we sorted her parents' things into bags for storage or donating.

Just as the sun was setting outside the window and Mary's resolve was wavering, there was a knock on the door. The surprise on her face melted into a smile as she saw Cormac in the doorway with wine glasses and a bottle in hand.

"I thought you were hiding out?" she asked, folding another one of her mother's tops into a pile before standing.

Cormac shrugged, handing her a glass before clearing some space on the dressing table. "Someone told me to get my ass out of bed."

She looked at me then, amusement sparkling in her eyes.

"I may or may not have sent little Luke on a mission with the babysitter." I chuckled, holding my hands up in defence.

Cormac mouthed thank you behind her back as he set about pouring the drinks. Wine wasn't my thing, but for

Mary's sake, I slipped away while we all worked on sorting through the rest of the alpha's thing before night fell.

I found myself zoning out of what I was doing to watch the two of them laughing and slagging each other about some family trip. Mary was throwing her head back with genuine laughter, and Cormac seemed more at ease than he had for weeks. Maybe they would be ok. It took guts to do this today. Any time Mary started to wallow, her brother would bring her round, stepping up to take care of her. I could see the alpha in him. Maybe he was too young, but he was his father's son and would be a great leader.

"Thanks again for doing this." Mary gestured to the tidied bags piling up with an apologetic half-smile that didn't quite reach her eyes.

I shrugged, kneeling down to start on one of the bedside lockers. "No problem, though I will consider you indebted to me and call on some giant favour someday."

"Yeah, probably to drive your drunken ass home some night." She rolled her eyes mockingly, tossing a T-shirt right at my face.

"Hey, I don't do that anymore!" I ducked just in time so that it hit Cormac instead, running a hand through my hair under my imaginary halo. "I'm a dad now."

Marys arched an eyebrow. "I'll believe it when I see it."

Before I could look to Cormac for back-up, he was already shaking his head and waving a white jacket as if it were a flag. "Nope, I'm Switzerland."

"You know you could just say Ireland, we're neutral too?" Mary challenged him, sounding more like herself.

He shrugged, leaning down to pull out the drawers of the locker on his side of the bed. "I never did pay attention in history."

Mary began one of her many rants about the importance of Irish history. We groaned, but neither of us interrupted her.

If this made Mary happy even for a few minutes, the least we could do was listen.

Letting her ramble, I shuffled through the items in the drawer, a mix of different nail care items that I had no clue what to do with, some old birthday cards, and concert tickets. This must have been their mother's side.

"What should I do with this?" I asked, still cleaning through the drawers with one hand while I waved about a flowery address book.

When no one answered, I sat back on my knees and looked across the bed to see Mary standing over Cormac. She was rigid and all colour had drained from her face. Both of them were staring intently at a page in his hand.

"Guys? What's wrong?"

I scrambled to my feet, tripping over the corner of the bed in my rush to get to them.

Cormac passed Mary the letter with silent tears rolling down his cheeks. She held the letter out, her hand shaking so much I had to hold the paper myself to read it clearly.

"It was hidden in my father's beside cabinet. He's always had a safe there and it's usually locked..."

I straightened out the paper. The letter was written in Luke's signature style, but the alpha's handwriting seemed rushed. He was always fantastic at speeches, yet this seemed forced and panicked.

Mary,

My sweetheart, first of all, please know that we love you and your brother more than anything in the world. All I wanted was to protect you, and I have failed. I fear that your mother and I are in danger. If you're reading this, the worst has happened.

I do not know who is responsible, but someone wants us out of the way and that puts you and your brother in danger too. Please, get to the bottom of this before it's too late. I'm sorry to place this burden on your shoulders, but it's up to you to save your brother. If they've come for us, he is next.

Love you, now and forever,

Mam and Dad x

My eyes scanned the pages, dread settling in the pit of my stomach. Something was off.

I looked up to see Mary watching me, tears glistening in her eyes. There were so many thoughts running through my mind. *When did he write this and why would someone kill the alpha?* It had been a car crash and the witches found no evidence of foul play, so the pack had no reason to suspect otherwise. But something about it had never sat right with me.

"It wasn't an accident," Mary said, placing a heavy hand on her brother's shoulder. "Our parents were murdered. Someone killed our alpha."

"This can't be real," Cormac mumbled, his voice thick with emotion. "Who would kill them?"

"We never would have found the letter if he hadn't given me a spare set of his office keys the day before the accident." Mary exhaled a shaky breath before continuing. With each word, her voice grew more certain. "He said it was in case of emergencies. I was just stoked he trusted me with something so big, but he was trying to protect us...."

I rubbed my forehead, trying to get my brain to kick in again. "We need to show this to someone."

"No," Mary snapped, taking the letter back and immediately folding it up carefully before putting it in her pocket. "No one can know about this."

She clung to it as if her life depended on it. Not only did it enclose important information, but it was the last message she had from her father.

"Everyone is a suspect," she whispered, staring at the letter as if it might give her an answer. When she looked up at me from under her lashes, there was a quiet determination in her eyes. "I need your help to figure this out. My dad is right. If they went after the alpha, Cormac is next."

CHAPTER 4

The afternoon sun filtered through the window, and the curtains gently swayed in the breeze. It was the perfect day for a birthday party—if I could ever get Luke into his clothes.

He tore around the bedroom butt-naked, teetering on his tiptoes most of the time. His favourite thing was to hang off the chest of drawers. Seeing me go white seemed to amuse him. So, I'd nailed it to the wall and child-proofed the entire room over the last week. Now he could skate around on the wooden floors to his heart's content until he inevitably fell on his bum.

Normally, I'd jump at the chance to play with him, but between Mary's revelation weighing on my mind and it being Laura's anniversary, I was in a weird headspace. Not to mention, it felt weird celebrating his birthday while there might be a murderer lurking in our pack.

Luke finally settled in his favourite spot; a colourful soft play mat stacked high with an army of teddies, a fire truck, and number blocks. You name it, he had it. I knew I was spoiling him a bit, but I couldn't help it. Despite my wrongdoings, he was a happy child who was always smiling and willing to share.

I grabbed him from behind, ignoring his wriggles and thrashing as I carried him to the bed. Holding him still with one hand, I reached across to grab a nappy.

"Daddy!" he squealed, tossing a block at me with uncanny precision.

It hit the side of my head and I winced. Luke erupted into a fit of giggles. One look at the cheeky grin Luke wore and all frustration dissipated. I caught the block and handed it back to a very amused toddler.

"Happy birthday mister. How are you growing up so fast?" I mused aloud, wrestling a pair of little jeans onto his kicking legs.

I could barely believe it had been two years since he came into my life—two years since I lost Laura. While in one sense it felt like a lifetime has passed, in another sense, time had flown by when it came to Luke growing up. From walking to talking, he was learning new things daily. As much as it hurt, it was impossible to dwell on what I had lost when he was so full of life. If it wasn't for my son, I'm not sure I would have been able to cope.

"There." I set Luke back down on the ground once he was changed and had shoes on. "That wasn't so bad, was it?"

Luke peered up at me, holding onto the edge of the mattress as he wobbled. He was the image of me with the mop of blonde hair, but his amber eyes matched his mothers, as did his mischievous streak. Within seconds, he had bolted back over towards his toys.

"Luke, we've gotta go."

When I hoisted him into my arms he cried out, desperately clinging onto a little toy car.

"It's your birthday party." I sighed, resting him on my hip as I wrestled the car from his hands, much to his dismay. "You are the birthday boy and you're gonna make so many new friends today."

He huffed, his bottom lip trembling.

"I guess you don't want all the presents waiting downstairs either then…"

That caught his attention.

Luke looked up at me from under his lashes with suspicion.

"Presents and cake, that sounds good, doesn't it?" I said cheerfully, walking out into the hallway and closing the door behind us. "Everyone is waiting for you."

"Grandad!"

"Yes, grandad will be there too." I shook my head, starting down the hall. That's when I saw what he was getting so excited about.

"Grandad!" Luke's face lit up at the sight of my father.

He wriggled in my arms until I relented and let him down. The moment his feet hit the ground, he took off towards my father who crouched down and scooped Luke into his arms.

Whatever my feelings about him, he had been at every milestone event, every birthday. When Laura died, he stayed in London for a month helping us adjust, even if much of that time was spent badgering me into coming home.

"Well if it isn't my favourite grandson. Happy birthday." My father teasingly moved the present out of Luke's reach before setting him down so he could run off and tear open the wrapping paper. He smoothed his hands on his pants and tapped his watch, his expression turning sour. "He's late for his birthday party."

I shook my head, brushing a hand through my hair. "It's fine, he's only a few minutes late. You should know children don't listen to timetables."

"You're too lenient with him." He tutted, then chuckled as he watched Luke unwrapping the present and squealing with happiness at his new toy. "Now, let's get you downstairs birthday boy."

Clutching his new toy, Luke happily ambled towards the staircase, his little fingers wrapped tightly around my father's hand. I ignored the sting, boxing the unwanted feelings away and trailed after them, picking up the trail of wrapping paper left in their wake.

Initially, when my father had suggested a birthday party, I wasn't too keen on the idea. Luke was still the new kid and I was still adjusting to being home, but when we stepped out into the gardens, the wide smile that lit up my son's face told me it had been the right decision. There were two picnic benches for the kids and longer tables for the adults, a giant wolf-themed bouncing castle set up, and a barbecue off to the side beside a table stacked high with plates and drinks.

I had to admit, I was surprised by the turnout. There were several kids and their parents, but it looked like most of the pack had joined in as well. Maybe they just wanted a reason to celebrate something good for a change.

"Did you do this?" I asked, watching Luke run off to join in a game of chasing with the other kids, his present left in the dust.

He nodded, an uncharacteristic smile warming his features. "With help from Aoife, Mary, and a few others."

Both of the girls were over beside the barbecue, and I was relieved to see that it was Mary rather than her little cousin in charge of the burgers. Anyone who dared interfere with her process got a dirty look that had them running in the opposite direction with their tail between their legs. She was the best cook in the pack—her mother had been the main chef in the kitchens before she died. Mary had definitely inherited her mother's skills. It was one of the few areas where the men weren't in charge.

"Thank you." Unsure of what to do, I settled for giving

my father's shoulder a light pat. "He needed this—I needed this."

My father nodded, his eyebrows quirking up in surprise. We didn't do affection. He opened his mouth to say something but for once in his life, he appeared to think better of it.

Watching the kids tumble on the bouncing castle and chase each other around in circles was sweet for a little while. I loved seeing Luke so happy, but I'd be a liar if I said the high-pitched screams, the yelling, and then the inevitable tears weren't getting on my nerves just a bit. Did that make me a bad father?

When it was time for food, there was absolute ructions trying to get everyone off the bouncing castle. It wasn't just the toddlers either. Some of the older kids were stubborn as hell. They only settled when they were ushered to the picnic benches and distracted with pizza, and burgers, and ketchup flying everywhere.

I did the rounds, trying to talk to everyone who turned up for my son's birthday. Between helping my dad in his practice and looking after Luke, I hadn't had much time to catch up with everyone. No one seemed to mind though, they welcomed me with open arms. It was interesting hearing what had been happening from different points of view, seeing who had kids, who didn't, and then there was the gossip of course.

An older woman called Liz, known for her razor-sharp tongue, was intent on giving me the low-down. She knew everything about every pack member. I remember when my friends and I were old enough to start dating or sneaking out, she was the one to avoid. If she caught you, the whole pack knew.

She was bending my ear about someone off dating a local, a normal *human*—scandalous, though I was barely paying attention at this point—when I caught sight of Darren over by the stack of drinks. He was tall with brown hair and a dark tan was visible on his bare arms from his trip abroad. I'd recognise the back of his giant head anywhere.

"Sorry Liz, do you mind if I go check on something?" I asked politely.

"Sure." She waved her hand in dismissal with a suggestive wink. "I can't keep a boy like you entertained for long."

I flashed her a lopsided grin, shuddering inside. "Thanks."

Darren was sorting through the bottles of juice and soft drinks, clearly looking for something stronger, if I knew him at all. I snuck up behind him and grabbed him by the shoulders. He jumped and spun to face me, the liquid in his plastic cup sloshing and spilling all over his hand.

"Tom! Mate, ever heard not to sneak up on someone?" Darren growled, the corners of his lips twitching in amusement. He shook his hand, grabbing a napkin to wipe it off. "Still as childish as ever then."

"Use your nose more." I teased, pouring a drink for myself and another for Darren. "I couldn't resist, sorry. You've always been so easy to scare."

Darren scowled but he couldn't disagree.

We had grown up together, joined at the hip right up until I went off to college. Darren hadn't been interested in college. He preferred working with his hands and went for an apprenticeship instead. When I was studying in Dublin, he often came to stay on campus with me at weekends. Once I moved to London for the PhD, we were still in close contact, but he could only come to visit every few months. After Luke was born, it was me who dropped the ball. Darren still called regularly to check in on me, so maybe now I could make it up to him.

"I've missed you man." Darren pulled me in for a hug, giving me a friendly slap on the back that sucked the air from my lungs. "Sorry I wasn't there for the funeral. I couldn't get back from Australia in time. I never expected something like that to happen while I was away."

"It was nice, for the most part. I didn't really stick around for most of it, just felt a bit too raw." I scuffed the toe of my runners on the grass. "How was backpacking?"

"It was good fun, met some of the Aussie packs. They're a good crowd." He shrugged, taking a long sip of his beer before continuing. "Once I heard about Luke's passing, it kind of put a dampener on things."

I nodded and we both took another swig of beer.

"How's being home?" he asked, his blue eyes sparking with sympathy.

"Difficult, same old same old. It's not quite as bad as I thought it would be."

"Well, I'm glad you're back mate." Darren reached out with his glass to clink it against mine and flashed me a warm smile, his voice growing serious. "I missed having my buddy around."

I returned the gesture, his sincerity catching me off guard. Darren was usually the joker.

"I—eh, I'm sorry about after... I know I didn't return your calls half the time..." I mumbled, rubbing the back of my neck.

Darren shook his head, waving his hand dismissively. "You were dealing with stuff; grief is a tricky thing. "How are you now?" he asked, his eyes searching mine.

I took a deep breath and exhaled slowly, giving the question some thought. "It still hurts. I don't think it will ever stop, but Luke keeps her alive for me. Being back here helps, I think."

"Being around your father helps?" Darren teased, back to his usual nature. "That's a new one."

"He's being..." I trailed off, searching for the right word to describe our weird relationship. "Nice. For him, I guess. I think he's trying, and he's good with Luke, even if he still treats me like a black sheep. Damien is still the favourite, obviously."

I felt petty even saying it, but Darren threw me a knowing look of agreement.

"Aye, he's always had a soft spot for that little creep." He glanced over his shoulder towards the bouncing castle. "I know your father has a bit of a thing with the mother and Nick isn't so bad, but I'll never understand what he sees in Damien."

It was common knowledge that my father and Damien's mother were in some kind of low-key relationship. It grossed me out though.

I followed Darren's eye-line to see Damien standing to one side of the bouncing castle. All of the kids were packed onto the picnic benches digging into the first round of food while Mary readied the second batch for the adults. Anyone who wasn't helping to keep the kids under control stood around in groups chatting, laughing, and drinking. And then there was Damien. Alone, with his arms folded across his chest and his signature brooding look shadowing his features. Nick was off talking to some of the younger guys like a normal person while his brother seemed to have withdrawn from everyone.

It wasn't that the pack shunned him or anything, he was just difficult to talk to. He had always been forceful with his opinions, but after his mother left and as he grew older, he became harder to reason with. He had a handful of friends, which was good, but so many people had told me he made them feel on edge. I used to think they were being slightly dramatic, but it was crystal clear since I had returned from London. The kid was a ball of fiery hatred. That's the only way I could describe it. He had no respect and flouted pack values—yet for some reason, my father idolised him.

Darren met my gaze, his lips thinning. "I'm telling you

dude, he's only gotten worse since you left for college. Even his friends talk about him behind his back."

"He's had a troubled childhood." I sighed, knocking back another mouthful of beer as if it would help.

"That's no excuse for the way he's turned out," Darren muttered, raising his hand to stop me before I could protest. "You can't blame your father either, you turned out just fine."

"I did?" I teased, the corners of my lips twitching.

He flashed me a lopsided grin. "Don't let it go to your head."

CHAPTER 5

B eing back in the surgery room felt good even if it wasn't a hospital. I'd had a handful of interviews, no call-backs yet, but I was optimistic. For now, my father's little practice would do the job. He had a good set-up in the main house on the first floor, so that outside visitors didn't get to nose around the house, and a back entrance for discretion. Being near the basement meant we could store supplies down there and set up a small operation room for the odd emergency. The surgery itself wasn't so bad. Bright, welcoming colours tinted the room, and my father's degrees hung framed on the walls. He kept the clutter to the adjoining room, my father's 'back office' of sorts—my main office for the foreseeable future until I could nail down my own job.

Knee deep in another job application, I was spaced out and staring intently at my laptop screen when I sensed my father walking up behind me.

"Filing those records away does not require you to be checking your emails." My father peered over my shoulder. "I thought we talked about this?"

He's like my bloody shadow.

Needless to say, I hadn't been getting more hugs recently and we had descended into our normal pattern of bickering.

"Sorry," I muttered, quickly closing down the tabs and snapping the laptop shut. "I just miss being on the ward."

He sighed, his greying eyebrows bunching together. "I'll see if I can put a word in, but there's plenty to be done here."

I motioned to the stacks of files in his office—paperless wasn't a thing here—and rolled my eyes. "Yeah, so much paperwork. You should really get a secretary."

"Who needs one when I have you?"

I shook my head, watching him disappear into the adjacent room to see another patient. There were only around sixty of us in the pack, but members from other packs came to visit him specifically. Between the odd knock a child got before their werewolf healing kicked in and pregnancies, he did alright.

Yet there I was, having been relegated to his walk-in filing cabinet.

My father kept telling me that I was overqualified, which didn't make me feel better about getting under his feet. He was the pack doctor, serving our pack and the handful of other Irish packs if they had an emergency. Sending werewolves to normal hospitals was never a good idea. With the recent advancements in technology, having our blood tested was a no go—the magical element fried the machines. Then there was the risk of a seriously injured werewolf passing out and shifting during the full moon or a claw extending at random when they were in too much pain. It was much simpler and better for all of us to treat problems internally.

The London pack had a similar plan going, except they had their own doctor stationed at one of the main hospitals. My wife's brother, that's how we met. I had been hoping to implement a similar system in Ireland and even suggested it to the alpha before he passed. As someone who was pushing for wolves to integrate with and adapt to the modern world, he thought the idea was fantastic. Unsurprisingly, my father wasn't keen.

A knock on the door distracted me from yet another application. The door handle rattled as whoever was outside tried to get in, but we usually kept it locked, especially if my father was in with patients.

"Give me one sec," I called out, walking over to the door and fiddling with the key until the lock clicked.

Creaking the door open, I was surprised to see the hallway outside empty. I stepped out to see a shadow disappearing around the corner, my nostrils flaring as I picked up a familiar scent.

"Shane?"

At the sound of his name, Shane reappeared, peeking his head around the corner. A large black hoodie dwarfed his frame. He was Darren's little brother and they were the spitting image of each other, but Shane was a bit smaller and dressed more rock-and-roll than Darren's gym rat style.

"I—uh, I thought your father might be around," Shane mumbled, toying with the end of his sleeve.

I shrugged, gesturing for him to come inside. "He's with a patient. I'm around?"

He hesitated for a moment before starting down the hallway and joining me in the surgery.

I closed the door behind us, noting how he jumped as the lock clicked, and took a stack of papers off a chair, placing it opposite my paper-ridden desk.

"Take a seat." I motioned to the seat opposite as I took my place behind the desk.

Shane gingerly lowered himself into the chair, immediately fidgeting so much he practically had to sit on his hands. One of the biggest things I had learned in my career as a doctor was that patients were rarely completely honest, so sometimes you had to pay attention to the smaller cues and coax the truth out of them to get to the bottom of the issue. This was especially true when it came to werewolves not wanting their business becoming pack gossip.

"Sorry my father is busy. What's up?"

It was obvious Shane wasn't here to see my father. Everyone knew he didn't work past four in the evening unless it was an emergency.

He nodded, swallowing nervously. "These rooms are soundproofed right?"

"Yeah, they have to be for patient confidentiality reasons," I explained, my brow creasing as I tried my best to come across as friendly as possible and put him at ease.

Being his older brother's best friend, I practically watched Shane grow up. I was there for his first drink; I even flew home for his twenty-first birthday. He was always a joker, brimming with confidence, yet he sat in front of me like a little kid who had been called to the principal's office.

Shane toyed with the loose threads on the leather chair, his gaze wandering around the room. "I think I'm in trouble."

"What kind of trouble?" I tried to keep my tone even as a long list of possibilities ran through my mind.

A wave of different expressions crossed his features as he warred with himself.

"Shane?" I prompted, leaning forwards with my elbows propped on the desk. "I won't be telling Darren, so you can tell me anything. I'm a doctor, it's my job to help. Whatever it is, whatever you've gotten yourself into, we can fix it."

He nodded, opening and closing his mouth several times before an actual word came out. "I've screwed up big time. I think my g—"

Before he could finish the sentence, there was a noise in the hall. I didn't pay any heed, but all colour drained from Shane's face.

"Relax," I murmured, motioning for him to continue.

The door handle creaked, followed by the office door swinging open as Damien entered the room without so much as knocking.

"Damien? What the hell?" I snapped, jumping to my feet and pointing towards the door. "Get out, I'm busy."

Shane noticeably stiffened, his shoulders tense as he rose from the chair, eyeing the adjoining door nervously as my father's shadow moved behind the tinted glass. "I better go."

You can still tell me what the problem is."

"Some other time."

"Shane, come on..." I pleaded, my sigh of frustration morphing into a growl as the adjoining door burst open and my father stepped into the room.

"What's going on here?" My father demanded, his demeanour changing when he caught sight of Darren's brother. "Ah Shane! What can I do for you? I don't think we had an appointment."

I scowled, rising from my father's chair. "*I* was dealing with him."

"This isn't your surgery though, is it?" My father grunted, looking to me briefly before zeroing in on Shane once more. "Is everything alright?"

Shane shook his head, retreating towards the exit. "I'm fine, I was just relaying a message for Darren."

"Looks like you're not busy after all, Tom." Damien's beady little eyes shone with amusement.

I kicked the leg of the desk in frustration, shooting Shane an apologetic grimace as he disappeared out the door, practically bolting down the hallway.

My father turned his attention to me, his eyes narrowed with that all too familiar expression of disapproval. "Why didn't you tell him to make an appointment?"

"I'm a doctor and he seemed anxious, so I thought it was

best to see him now. I was getting somewhere before you rocked up."

"You should have had him make an appointment," he repeated, his tone edging too close to the one of chastising a child. "Don't forget that they are *my* patients."

I scowled, stuffing papers I needed into my laptop bag. "I didn't study and train for years just to be a glorified receptionist."

Not treating patients was really getting to me. Having gone from the fast-paced hospital environment to filing had taken its toll. It was like a real-life game of snakes and ladders. Every time I thought we made some progress, he'd pull a stunt like this and I'd be back at square one.

"Did you get all the filing done?" He asked, ignoring my point entirely.

"Sorry to break up the domestic," Damien cut in, straightening up and fixing his tie. "I need to talk to you, Fiachra, if you're not too busy putting Tom on the naughty step."

Smug git.

I grit my teeth and didn't take the bait.

"What is it?"

"Nothing serious, just some pack business." Damien shrugged, shooting me a pointed look. "Private business."

Damien tried to keep his blaze mask up, but the tension in his shoulders and clipped tone gave him away, and I couldn't help wondering what had him so wound up.

I stood my ground, lingering by my father's desk just to annoy Damien. Call me childish, but I was sick of being pushed around.

Eventually, my father looked up and rolled his eyes with a resigned sigh. "Tom, can you give us privacy?"

"Sure."

Just as I turned on my heel to leave, my father handed me a pile of files.

"Put these away before you go, then you can go for today." He placed the hefty stack of paperwork in my hands and waved a dismissive hand towards the exit.

The tell-tale tone of his voice told me the conversation was over.

I took one look at the filing cabinet and decided to just dump the stack of files on top. My father could deal with them later. And if that was too much, maybe he should hire a receptionist because I was done being his lackey. I was overqualified and didn't have the patience. As I left the office, I lost my composure and slammed the door behind me for good measure, hearing my father mutter profanities as the glass rattled in my wake.

CHAPTER 6

Between Luke's birthday and finding that letter, the week had flown by. Amidst all the madness, my routine with Luke was the only thing keeping me sane. My favourite time of the day was always tucking him into bed. When I had been working in London, shift work meant I missed out on so many precious moments. Being able to read him bedtime stories and watch him snuggle his little teddy as tiredness took over was priceless.

He wasn't a fan of the cot, so my father had helped me pick out a cute little kid's bed with a side rail, so Luke couldn't accidentally fall out, to put in the corner near my bed. It was painted to look like a car and had patterned bed covers to match. He thought it was the best thing ever and wanted to live in it.

"And the little bear promised he would never sneak out again," I whispered, finishing one of Luke's favourite books just in time.

His eyelids fluttered closed and his breathing slowed. He clutched his wolf teddy in the crook of one arm as he slipped off to sleep.

I watched him for some time, gently stroking his hair and smiling to myself.

There was a light knock on the door and Luke stirred but didn't wake.

Placing the book down the small bedside locker, I walked over to the door and nudged it open to see Mary in the dim hallway, impatiently dancing from one foot to the other.

"What's up?"

She pressed her hands together in a silent clap of excitement. "I have it, I have some proof."

Even in my sleepy state, I knew she could only be talking about one thing. I tiptoed back into the room and grabbed a baby monitor before following her down the hall and up the winding staircase to the top floor.

Mary led the way into her room, and I'm not sure what I was expecting, but it wasn't this.

The ivory walls of her bedroom were plastered from floorboard to roof with magazine and newspaper cuttings of every shape and size, with one wall serving as a make-shift whiteboard. Scribblings in sharpie and harsh red lines joined up different snippets, some circled, some with question marks. I had no idea where it started or ended, only that she must have gone through every newspaper article and official report she could get her hands on. It looked like something out of Criminal Minds.

I let out a low whistle, turning slowly in a circle to take in the full extent of obsessed she had gone to. Finally, I turned to Mary, eyebrows raised in question.

She didn't seem the least bit fazed.

"I've been looking into the accident." She shrugged, as if that was the only explanation needed.

"I can see that."

She folded her arms across her chest defensively. "What? What else am I supposed to do?"

"Okay, show me what you've found," I relented, gesturing to the mass of information papering the wall.

Mary walked over to the whiteboard that had a line drawn down the middle and two lists scrawled on either side.

"I went through every single article that was published on the accident and then compared them to the official reports." She pointed to the various snippets pinned up and then a section that looked like typed up extracts from formal write-ups. "I didn't expect to find much, but I noticed straight away they don't add up."

"The media is never accurate," I mused aloud, earning myself an icy glare.

She planted her feet firmly on the ground, clutching the marker in her hand as if she might launch it at my head. "I know that. How much of a coincidence is it that they all report the *exact* same story then?"

"It would be unusual for them to be identical," I conceded.

"They are."

I frowned, walking closer to the wall plastered in cuttings and read a few headlines. They varied slightly, but when it came to the main details reported, Mary was right; they all said the exact same thing.

"They claim my parents were not found until the early hours of the morning by a random passer-by, and according to the paramedics, were already dead when they arrived." She gripped the marker in her hand so tightly the plastic began to splinter, emotion making her voice waver. "That *both* of them were impaled by a tree when the car crashed into it. Catastrophic, car was a wreck."

"The pack probably had to control the narrative?"

"We don't revert to our wolf form when we die," she retorted, making me feel like any suggestion I had, she had already thought of, especially if she had been spilling over this for days. "There's no need to control what was published unless they were hiding something: the truth."

I followed her over to the make-shift whiteboard. The first list was all the identical facts used in the different media reports of the accident, but she was already on the second list.

"These are facts from the official reports and documentation that don't match with the media reports," she said, underlining the list on the right with the marker. "The time of death on the death certificate is down as ten-twenty at night."

"Wait, the death certificate?"

I'd been stuck filing for days and on one occasion, when boredom took hold, I had gone looking for the death certificate to satisfy my curiosity. When it wasn't there, I'd put it down to still being with the coroner or something.

"I took the death cert from your dad's office. Most of it is redacted, but not the time of death," Mary said with a shrug as she produced the document from one of her many folders.

"There's no way my father let you dig around in the office." I frowned, taking the cert in hand to examine it. "He'd go mad."

She produced a set of keys, the metal jiggling as she waved it about. "I found these when we were cleaning out my parent's stuff. Skeleton keys for the manor."

I should have been surprised, but I was too busy reading through the rest of the list, my mind kicking into gear when I realised she had actually found something. Not only was the time of death hours before any of the media claimed they were found but the medical statement was redacted. The media said they were impaled by a tree, which wouldn't kill a werewolf, unless the tree had pierced both their hearts directly. Seriously injured, yes, but they would have survived. There was no fallen tree reported in the police report, only that the car crashed into it head on.

When I was in London, I treated a good few humans injured in car crashes. There had been one werewolf, a young lad who thought he was a street racer and wrapped his car around a tree. He had a collapsed lung, some broken ribs, a dislocated shoulder, a snapped tibia, and was pretty cut up overall. By the time he came to me, the bones were already trying to heal. I just had to set them and help the collapsed lung a bit. When he showed me a picture the next day, there was nothing left of the car except for a mangled chassis. The chance of both of Mary's parents dying the same way in an accident was beyond the realms of likelihood.

Werewolves aren't invincible. There are poisons that can kill us but using extreme force and impaling us so that we can't heal does the trick as well. Silver isn't a myth either. We die of old age but have a slightly longer lifespan than a human. The easiest way to kill a werewolf is to rip their heart out.

I turned to Mary, blurting out the question in the least tactful way. "Did you prepare your parents for the funeral? Did you see them?"

"Of course I did. It was the last thing I could do for them," she snapped, and this time she did fling the marker full force at my head.

"Sorry!" I ducked just in time to let the marker ricochet off the wall behind me. "I know it's a horrible question, but how did they look?"

She bent to pick up the marker, pausing for thought. "Your dad had cleaned them up a bit already. Their faces looked normal, but their chests were bandaged up. There were cuts and bruises I had to hide with make-up."

"Their chests were bandaged?" I asked, trying to keep her on track.

"Yeah, from the ribs up, which did kind of make sense at the time because that's what hit the steering wheel."

I frowned, forming a picture in my mind about what I'd

expect to see from the kind of blunt force trauma that was reported. "When you were dressing them, was there any bruising on the abdomen or above the bandages across their collarbone and shoulders?"

"Dad had bruising above the bandages, mam not so much." Her voice grew distant, her eyes glassy as if she was reliving the memory.

"No cuts?"

Mary shook her head. "Just bruising and little cuts here and there."

If a tree had impaled them through their hearts, they would have died instantly, giving their body no chance to heal. Their ribcage would have been crushed and there would have been a lot more damage than Mary was describing. In fact, they would have been in no state to be displayed on the pyre or to be seen by their daughter.

My heart started working double time, and I felt that tiny sense of dread that had lingered since Damien's speech multiplied.

"The media reports are fake, but that's not what worries me. It sounds like the car crashed, but that's not what killed them," I said, meeting Mary's heavy gaze and swallowing before I forced the last words out. "From what I can tell, it looks like someone tore their hearts out. The question is, who?"

Mary looked up from the letter, her gaze troubled but her tone was certain. "It had to be someone he trusted. This was definitely an inside job. Someone in this pack killed our alpha."

CHAPTER 7

When Darren rocked by asking to meet up for coffee just as I was locking up the surgery after a quiet Saturday morning, it was a welcome relief. Only time spent with Luke seemed to cheer me up, and even he was booked out for the afternoon on a play date. Spending the past week with Mary looking for answers had taken its toll, so chilling out with a friend without so much hanging over my head would be nice. I could try to be normal for a while.

Darren was waiting in his car out front, a flashy bright red Audi that turned all the girls' heads. He honked the horn, flashing me a lopsided grin.

"Impatient much?" I joked, sliding into the passenger seat and shutting the door just as Darren floored the accelerator and sped down the driveway.

He shrugged, locking the wheel as he swung out onto the road. "I just thought you'd want a break from the whole situation."

Watching the manor disappear in the rearview mirror allowed the tension pent up in my shoulders and neck to release a fraction. Darren didn't even know the full extent of the *situation*, but he was right, I needed a break.

"So, where are we headed?" I sighed in content as I settled into the leather seats and watched the countryside flash by. "The Dark Night?"

He shook his head, and I caught his jaw twitch out of the corner of my eye.

"Nah." He kept his focus on the road. "I thought we'd try be normal for once, Sha—uh, I mean Mary, told me about some new coffee they have in that café on Grafton Street. I thought we could try that."

He was a bad liar. Mary hated coffee chains, and she'd never have recommended Bewley's. It might have been a national treasure, but she much preferred a home brew.

Darren was holding the steering wheel just that little bit too tight, his easy breezy demeanour fading in and out like the wind. He was nervous. I'd seen it a few times, mainly when we were young teenagers and Darren was still learning the ropes and finding out how to play the field with girls. One girl in particular used to turn the man who was never loss for words mute. But we weren't kids anymore, and I was his best mate, so why the nerves?

Fields lining the roads slowly faded, first to large estates on the outskirts of the city, and then to larger buildings. The River Liffey split the city in two, joined by bridges bustling with tourists. I inhaled deeply, smelling car fumes along with thousands of different scents hanging in the air. The mountains were my home, but I loved Dublin. We were lucky that the pack territory was barely thirty minutes outside of the city. Only in Ireland would you have such a shift.

Darren parked in the underground car park of the office building Luke had rented for the legal company he was setting up before he passed.

"So, are you gonna tell me what's up?" I asked as we

walked across one of the many bridges lining the river, enjoying the feeling of the winter sun on my face. "Or do I have to bully it out of you?"

He chuckled, though it didn't quite ring true. "I'll tell you when we get there."

We fought our way through the crowds in Temple Bar, a popular area on the south bank of the River Liffey. Tourists poured out of the famous pub of the same name onto the cobbled streets. When we ducked out onto the Grafton Street, it was just as busy. Buskers lined the side of the street, set up outside shop fronts with guitars. It was a weekend, of course the city was buzzing.

By the time we reached Bewley's, Darren had barely spoken two words. When he had asked to meet up, I was expecting a nice chat with my friend, but talking to him was like trying to pull fangs. We took a seat nestled between the window and the balcony overlooking the ground floor on the second floor. He spent half the time staring into his coffee like he was reading tea leaves and the other half checking a large golden-framed clock that hung above the staircase.

I was pretty much talking to myself.

Only when the main door opened, and a familiar scent reached us did Darren's attention spark. He looked up from his coffee cup, and I followed his gaze to see a couple walk in. Seconds later Shane came into full view. The only wolf scent I detected was his, the girl was almost definitely human. Darren's brother left the girl to order, slowly making his way up the stairs to join us, wringing his hands and turning back every two seconds to check on her.

"Hey Shane." Darren stood to greet him, motioning to the seat next to him. "You're late."

The icy tone to his voice caught me off guard, and I wasn't the only one.

Shane's shoulders visibly slumped. "I'm sorry, there was traffic."

"No traffic when we drove in," Darren muttered, picking up a little teaspoon and stirring his coffee, slowly destroying the pretty little pattern they'd made on top. The novelty was lost on him.

"It's fine." I scooted one seat across and patted the spot next to me in a poor attempt to cut through the tension.

Instead of taking the seat offered, Shane quickly retreated with his tail between his legs back down the stairs. I could see him helping the girl with the tray, giving her a tender kiss on the cheek to take it away. I could only assume she was his girlfriend. Another woman had joined them, pulling Shane's girlfriend into a reassuring embrace before following them up the stairs.

As they neared us, my suspicions were confirmed. Both girls were human and that was fine. Plenty of wolves had human friends in recent years. It was still kind of new, but I was open to it. We all needed to integrate, and it was becoming the norm in places like London. What I was not prepared for was the distinct cloud of hormones I picked up.

The girl Shane had a protective arm wrapped around was pregnant.

The brothers shared a look, Darren wearing a thunderous expression. I watched their silent exchange, trying to decipher what the hell I'd been dragged into. Shane turning up at the office that time now made sense, he must have been looking for advice. Darren didn't appear surprised—he was furious. His brother must have confided in him about the pregnancy, but reality is a lot harder to swallow.

"This is Gráinne." Shane, who looked as if he might crumble under his brother's stare set his shoulders and pulled her closer to him. He smiled fondly as he introduced the girlfriend before gesturing to the friend that stood beside them. "And this is her best friend, Helena. Don't worry, she knows the full story."

Both girls shifted awkwardly, and Gráinne sidled closer to Shane, if that was possible. She was so close she was practically hiding behind him. Helena was less timid with fiery curls and green cat-like eyes that held my attention just a little bit too long. Calmly folding her arms across her chest, she nodded pointedly towards the empty chairs, clearly expecting an invitation to sit down.

I wasn't sure how I felt about Shane involving the friend unnecessarily, but Gráinne was terrified, and I couldn't really blame her for needing moral support.

Darren didn't look like he could get a word out, and if he did, he'd probably put his size nines in it.

"Nice to meet you," I said, my lips curving in what I hoped was a warm smile as I pulled out the chair nearest me. "Please, sit down."

Gráinne's shoulders sagged with relief. Shane placed the tray down on the table, the coffee sloshing around the cups, and held a seat out for Gráinne before planting himself in between his girlfriend and his brother. Helena sat opposite her best friend, beside me. I caught the light scent of jasmine as her hair moved.

I wasn't sure if I was brought along as moral support or some kind of referee to stop Darren killing his brother. Either way, it was obvious that he wasn't going to start the conversation and Shane looked ready to jump out the window, so it was left up to me to put everyone out of their misery.

"So... This is unexpected, but I'm really happy for both of you." I glanced around the table at our unusual little group and trying to find the best way to get them all talking. "When is the baby due?"

They shared a little look, and she laid a protective hand over her stomach. "June."

That gave us just under five months to figure out a plan.

Darren watched the exchange with his lips set in a thin line.

Shane was in his early twenties, barely halfway through his apprenticeship, and entirely reliant on the pack and his family. While they were tolerating pack members dating humans and sleeping around on the side, I wasn't sure they were ready for this. Accepting a human into the pack was a big deal, impossible even. Cormac had a kind heart, but did he have enough sway to convince the other members to accept a human and their child?

CHAPTER 8

An icy silence had descended on our table and it showed no sign of thawing. Darren stared at his brother and Gráinne with a mixture of emotions, the main one being anger. Helena shifted beside me and the café noises seemed to fade into the background.

I was about to tell them how great it was when Darren found his voice.

"Why didn't you tell me before now? You didn't even have the guts to tell me in person, and when I ask you to meet, you need back up?"

Shane swallowed, his jaw clenched. "I brought Gráinne because she has a right to be here. We are a couple. I was trying to figure out a plan."

"And the plan is? You're a kid Shane, how did you get yourself into this mess?" he snapped, throwing his hands up in the air in frustration.

Heads all around the café turned towards us and Gráinne shrank back, shooting her friend a desperate look. She was out of her depth; they both were. Darren's short fuse wasn't going to help matters. He'd pulled me out of many a confrontation, but now it was my turn to stop him crossing a line he'd regret.

"It's not a mess," I said firmly, trying to give what I hoped was a reassuring smile. "Unplanned, maybe, but that's not uncommon."

Darren growled, shooting his brother a nasty glare. "Ever heard of wrapping it?"

"Condoms break," Helena cut in.

I turned to look at her, expecting to see some element of fear in her eyes, but she wasn't fazed in the slightest even though she knew he was a werewolf losing his cool. I didn't have long to admire her confidence because Darren gripped the edge of the table and looked ready to flip it.

"You stay out of this. I don't even get why you're here." Darren growled at Helena, losing his non-existent patience.

"I'm her best friend, and I'm hardly going to let her meet a bunch of werewolves without me."

Darren rolled his eyes dismissively and turned back to the couple, his tone souring. "Do you realise what you have done? This baby could be a hybrid. How could you let that happen?"

Gráinne was staring at me and her friend, desperation shining in her eyes as they began to water. The poor girl was scared out of her wits. I wondered if she had even known Shane was a werewolf before the baby thing happened.

"When a mammy wolf and a daddy wolf—" Helena flashed a vicious grin at Darren, using a sing-song voice.

Darren turned on the gutsy redhead, eyes blazing. "She isn't a wolf though, is she? That's the whole problem."

I kicked him under the table, noticing that there were far too many heads turning our way. "Both of you cut it out, or we'll have to take this conversation to somewhere more suitable, and I don't think that's a good idea."

"It's fine for me, I'm not a human." Darren shrugged, sulking like a stubborn child.

I shot him a warning look. Having this conversation in such a public place might have been a safe option for the girls, but it was dangerous for us wolves.

"Look, we didn't plan this, but I'm not putting Gráinne on a boat to England." Shane leaned in closer, his jaw set and his tone final. "We are having that baby. I didn't ask for your permission, I asked for your help. You're my brother, and I need you to make sure I can keep this baby and my fiancé safe."

I groaned and buried my face in my hands. Darren's expression had begun to soften right up until Shane decided to drop the ring thing. Then all hell broke loose.

"You're fucking what?" Darren growled, leaping out of his chair and reaching across the table to grab his brother by the collar. "Do you have a death wish?"

The table jerked, plates sliding off and smashing onto the ground by their feet. Gráinne squealed and leaped out of her chair, rushing to Helena's side, tears streaming down her face.

By the time I skirted around the table and had a hand on the two guys, they were holding one another by the throat and wrestling back and forth, spitting insults at each other. I could feel the eyes of every single human in the café on us.

"Cut the crap, both of you!" I yelled, trying to pry Darren's hands off his brother but his grip was iron clad.

Beside us, Helena wrapped a protective arm around her friend, glaring daggers at Darren's back as he wrestled with his brother, though she looked torn between looking after Gráinne and knocking seven shades out of the two guys.

Darren's eyes flashed silver and Gráinne gasped as his claws began extending.

"Shit," I cursed, grabbing Darren by the shoulders and dragging both of them towards the stairs.

A waiter came up the stairs, a scrawny kid that couldn't have been much older than eighteen. His eyes widened as he caught sight of the fight. The poor guy knew he wouldn't be able to break this up.

I shot the waiter an apologetic smile as I hauled the two brothers apart, shoving them down the stairs as they threw the odd punch. They were still scrapping when they spilled out onto the street, but I didn't let them stop until I had pushed and pulled them into a nearby alleyway where they could kick the crap out of each other without exposing us completely.

Gráinne followed us, supported by Helena, her freckled complexion now deathly pale as she watched them fight. I guess it was one thing to see Shane all fluffy and playful, and another to see two werewolves fighting in their human form. At least they couldn't shift at the moment. That would send her over the edge.

"Are you done being idiots?" I demanded, standing between the two brothers and the girls.

The two brothers shared a defeated look and nodded, both doubled over and panting. Darren's T-shirt was torn along the neckline and he had the beginnings of a black eye on one side. Shane didn't look much better, rubbing his jaw and wincing. His shirt collar was hanging on by a thread.

"Good." I ignored their protests as I grabbed one arm each and forced them to shake hands. "Now, apologise for scaring the girls and we can all talk about this like adults."

We needed some space, so I marched all of them to the middle of Stephen's Green, a large park at the end of the main street. In late January, it was almost empty. The earlier sunshine had been replaced by the cool winds which had driven people inside. Darren could scream to his heart's content. If any humans heard him talking about werewolves, they would assume he was a junkie.

"Now." I stopped beside one of the old stone monuments with benches, perching on one of the low walls. "Let's try this again."

Darren sat beside me nursing one of his wrists. Neither had done enough damage they couldn't heal from. As for what was said and words that couldn't be taken back, that might take longer to fix.

Shane cleared his throat, wrapping a protective arm around his fiancé's waist and facing his brother with a renewed sense of confidence.

"I came to you for advice, not because I needed any more pressure or a black eye. We are well aware that this baby could be a hybrid, that's why I need help," Shane said, keeping his gaze firmly fixed on his brother. "I don't know if the pack will accept us, but I can't just hop on a bus and disappear into the night. I love my pack, my family."

As he hammered each word home, it slowly chipped away at Darren's resolve. He shifted on the wall, and I caught the slightest hint of a tear glistening in the corner of his eye. He wasn't angry at his little brother, he was angry at the situation, all fuelled by fear for his brother and the unborn child. It was common knowledge that hybrids were often treated like outcasts.

I could hear Gráinne holding her breath, clutching Shane's arm as she waited on the reaction. Little did she know, Darren had one of the biggest hearts around, she just wasn't seeing the best side of him. Despite what Shane might have told her, I wasn't sure she understood the gravity of this situation.

"Will the kid definitely be a hybrid?" Helena piped up, giving her friend's shoulder a sympathetic pat.

Helena's piercing eyes were fixed on me, along with everyone else's. I sighed, rubbing the back of my neck. This wasn't my area of expertise, and since it hadn't been studied enough, I didn't want to say the wrong thing.

"From what I've seen while working in London, and what I've heard, if it's a girl, it's pretty much guaranteed to be a hybrid. I'm not sure what the deal is with boys. I've only ever heard of female hybrids," I explained, knowing by the way Gráinne's bottom lip began to tremble that it wasn't the answer they wanted.

"We won't know until our scan next week. I didn't want to know... but now we have no choice." Gráinne clutched her friend's arm, panic rising in her voice.

"Either way, the pack will struggle to accept you and the child." Darren puffed out a loud sigh, clearly on the same wavelength as me.

Gráinne didn't seem to mind the idea of that too much. She appeared more concerned about trying to raise a child that had a side she could never understand. A human boy would be the best possible outcome.

Shane, Darren, And I shared a knowing look. Judging by the distinct mix of hormones we werewolves could smell, we could tell this would be a baby girl. Shane would have to break the news at some point, but this was not the time.

"We'll figure this out," I promised, trying to force some sense of belief into my words. "We will come up with something."

Shane and Gráinne nodded, their lips curving ever so slightly as they visualised the possibility of living happily ever after in their heads. I wasn't so sure that dream fit in well with our world.

The breeze picked up, a subtle hint for us to head home. I wanted to see Luke, and the others needed some time to think, especially the happy couple. I think Darren needed a drink.

Darren and his brother hugged it out, slapping each other's backs and muttering apologies to one another. He even gave Gráinne a gentle hug, and while she still was wary of her fiancé's brother, the smallest of smiles curved her lips.

I watched the exchange, standing beside Helena, shifting awkwardly from one foot to the other. Seeing their brotherly love was a sombre reminder of what a shit-show my own family was.

"Thank you," Helena said, her voice so quiet I barely caught her words in the wind.

"For what?"

She turned to me, those emerald eyes of hers making my breath catch in my throat. "For calming Darren down, stopping Gráinne from bolting out of here. This would have been a mess without you."

"I'm not sure I did much good. Darren was always going to lose his cool."

Helena shook her head, her fiery curls rustling with the movement. "You made a big difference. Darren respects you, as does Shane. It makes Gráinne feel better about the whole situation."

I rubbed my brow, uncomfortable with being painted as some kind of saviour.

"Relax." Helena's tone grew playful, a mischievous glint sparking in her eyes. "I'm not saying you can fix this, but you sure make it a hell of a lot less scary for Gráinne. Shane said you were a doctor."

Can she read my mind? I sniffed, doubting my skills for a moment. *Nope, just an incredibly perceptive human.*

Helena had this weird effect on me. She made me feel like my old self, as if I wasn't just a father, but I was still me. She was fearless, even when surrounded by paranormal creatures she must have thought only existed in fiction, with a sharp tongue and a fierce determination to protect her friend. I couldn't help but admire her, and I found myself not wanting to leave.

What if I never see her again?

Helena turned to me and held out her hand. "Give me your phone."

I frowned but didn't question her methods, handing over

my brick of a device my father insisted I carry in case of emergencies. At the same time, she handed me her own phone.

"Give me your number, just in case there's an emergency."

The screen on her phone was open on the add contacts screen, so I punched in my number as directed and hit save on the dull green screen, hoping I'd remembered it correctly. By the time I was finished, Helena was holding out my phone and Gráinne was back by her side, eyeing her friend curiously.

"Done." I handed her phone back, offering Gráinne who seemed a lot less nervous, a small smile.

To my surprise, Helena stepped forwards and threw her arms around my neck, pulling me in for a big hug. I returned the gesture, my senses overwhelmed by the scent of her hair, and the sound of her beating heart, and how she felt in my arms. Something that I thought was dead and buried sparked in me, and I felt blood rush to my cheeks.

"Call me," Helena said softly, her voice barely a whisper.

All too soon, the embrace was over, and Helena was back beside her friend, the two linking arms and turning to leave alongside Shane.

Darren joined me, a cheeky smirk lighting up his features. "What was all that about?"

I shook my head and glanced down at my phone and Helena's number, my mind reeling not for the first time that day.

"I have no idea," I mumbled, heat creeping up my neck.

"You better call her." Darren chuckled, clapping me on the back with a chuckle. "I've been on the other end of that temper of hers. Don't make a girl like that wait around, or you'll regret it."

For the first time since Laura had passed, I think I had a crush.

CHAPTER 9

Working with my father had become increasingly difficult since Mary found the redacted death cert. We still weren't sure it was him and despite wanting to confront him, I was scared of hearing the truth. He had always been moody and outspoken, but I couldn't picture him as a killer. As much as he had disliked Luke, he respected the pack hierarchy. He was old fashioned like that.

I glanced at the clock for the hundredth time that day. It was almost four in the afternoon and my father had insisted he needed to leave in time for a meeting. I was just looking forwards to getting rid of him.

Luke pottered over to me, waving an old stethoscope he had found in my face. "Dadddyyyyyy!"

"What have you got there, mister?" A smile tugged at the corners of my lips as I pulled him onto my lap.

He laughed, poking me with the wrong end to listen to my heartbeat. Aoife's mother was the pack childminder, but she was off on a trip, so I'd had to bring Luke to work. I didn't mind one bit, he brightened the place up and made the day fly by, especially when he was intent on tearing everything down. I spent most of the day running around after him.

The tell-tale noise of the door closing next door told me my father had finally pushed that last client out the door.

I sat Luke down with one of his toy cars, gathered up two envelopes in my hand and rapped lightly on the door.

My father had been kept busy all day by a callout to deal with a werewolf that got into beef with a Fae and ended up the worse for it, so I never got around to giving him the post. He was very particular about it going straight to him. The one day I'd opened a generic looking letter he'd taken the ear off me, and I wasn't risking another argument over something stupid.

He didn't answer, so I opened the door to find him rushing around muttering about his keys.

"I have your post." I placed one small envelope and a chunky one that looked like a file he might have requested or something on his desk. "The big one was stamped confidential."

My father spun to look at me, his cheeks flushed. "Have you seen my keys?"

I frowned, pointing to the set of keys hanging by the door. "Those?"

"Yes," he snapped, grabbing the keys off the hook before pulling on his suit jacket. "I don't have time for this."

"It looks important," I said with a shrug, retreating towards the door.

He was clearly in a mood.

Scowling, my father shot me a warning look before ripping the larger brown envelope open while muttering. "It's probably just junk."

As soon as he pulled the pile of papers out an inch, he took one look of them and tossed the envelope and its contents into his desk drawer before slamming it shut and locking it for good measure.

"Is everything okay?" I ventured.

My father's scowl deepened, his face turning a dark shade of beetroot. He glowered at me as if I'd just pissed in his cornflakes. "It's fine, I have to go now."

Luke waddled over to me, running the car up and down the wall and making engine noises.

"Uh..." I frowned, tilting my head as I watched him gather his things in a flurry of movement. "It doesn't look fine."

"Enough." He snatched his umbrella up before heading straight out the door and slamming it behind him so hard I thought it might come off the hinges.

Luke jumped at the noise, his bottom lip trembling. I scooped him into my arms with a sigh as my father's angry footsteps echoed down the hall. I was confused as hell. He always had a temper and a perpetually grumpy demeanour when it came to me, but I'd never seen him in such a hurry to go somewhere. Whatever this meeting was had really lit a fire under his ass, and that envelope was gasoline.

His strange behaviour was doing nothing to dissuade my worries of his involvement in whatever happened to the alpha.

The clock ticking in the background was a constant reminder that I should just finish up, but something didn't feel right.

I stared at my father's desk for a long time, trying to talk myself out of it. Curiosity killed the cat and all that, but it got the better of me.

Setting Luke down, I walked over the desk and gave one of the drawers a shake to see if it would come loose. This wasn't some antique desk; this thing had more drawers and compartments than you could need. It was overkill, but my father was an organisation freak.

The drawer wouldn't budge, but my misspent youth had taught me a few useful skills. I rooted around on his desk until I found what I wanted among his stationary collection.

"Hold this," I said, handing Luke a box of paperclips.

I felt bad including him in my little escapade, but the grin on his face told me he enjoyed being involved.

It took me a few minutes with a paperclip, and despite my rusty skills I got the top drawer open. The first drawer was full of useless paperwork like bills, and an address book that probably had a few dodgy contacts in it. There was no way I'd know who was who. I jiggled around with the second lock and the second drawer popped open. Smiling to myself and feeling just a little bit badass that I was getting to rifle through his stuff, I took out the large envelope that had my father so wound up.

Bingo.

Slouching in his chair, I emptied the contents of the envelope on the desk and pulled Luke onto my lap.

He ran his car over the papers while I tried to read.

The cover letter had a government stamp and a hospital letterhead, mixed in with something about the police, but it was the names listed that caught my eye: Luke and Marion McKenna.

I tossed the letter aside and started reading through the pages that followed, my heart beginning to thunder in my chest.

It was the full death cert. Not only that, but it had a complete medical examination attached which clearly stated that the cause of death was violent trauma to the chest, resulting in the removal of their hearts. Their rib cages had been splintered around the area of the removed organ and any bruising and impact injuries as a result of the car crash were pre-mortem. Clear proof this was a werewolf killing and should have been investigated by the witches. Removing a werewolf's heart—especially an alpha's—was no accident. The cause of death was down as murder.

"Daddy?" Luke's hazel eyes were wide with worry as he poked my arm.

I shook my head in an attempt to clear it, ruffling Luke's head to reassure him. "I'm fine, it's okay."

But it wasn't, nothing was all right. Everything was a mess.

Why did my father ask for this? Or was he down as next of kin? Was he just part of covering this up to hide our existence from the human world, or was this something more?

As the shock began to pass, I sprang into action. My father clearly didn't want me seeing this, so I lifted Luke down and put the pages back in the envelope, placing things back exactly as they were before shutting each of the drawers.

I locked up as fast as I could, my clammy hands fumbling with the keys as I ushered Luke out of the surgery.

Luke slipped his little hand in mine, but he couldn't keep up with my pace and I couldn't wait. I scooped him into my arms and speed walked down the hallway as fast as I could without flagging someone that something was up, though I was sure my facial expression didn't keep up the 'nothing is wrong' pretence. I was heading straight for the kitchens to tell Mary what I'd found.

The noise of laughter drifted towards me as I passed the staircase, followed by a loud crash. I frowned, both mine and Luke's head snapping towards the source of the noise. It was definitely coming from the back of the house. More laughter rang out, a rich laugh that was just like our old alpha's.

I set Luke down on the ground, a small smile ghosting my lips as he wrapped his little fingers around one of mine. Slowly, I walked with him towards the dining room, my adrenaline slowly dissipating as I recognised more of the voices. No foreign scents stood out.

Rapping on the dining room door, the source of the noise, I nudged a nervous Luke behind my legs. He didn't protest, gripping onto my knee and staying unusually quiet.

When no one answered, I twisted the locked doorknob and forced the door open with little effort. Inside, Cormac and a few of his friends were scattered around the table and a layer of smoke swirled in the air, the distinct smell of weed filling my nostrils. All of them stared at me with a mixture of apprehension and an unhealthy sense of inflated self-importance.

"What the hell is going on here?" I demanded, the harshness of my voice waking a few of the lads out of their drug induced state.

Silence followed. I felt Luke shrink back and reached behind me to pat his head in reassurance, keeping my narrowed eyes fixed on the warped bachelor party before me.

Cormac sat at the head of the table, a party hat with the word 'Alpha' scribbled on it in marker lopsided on his head. His eyes were bloodshot and unfocused, his unbuttoned shirt hanging off one shoulder. Gone was the man I thought might have been starting to come to grips with his responsibility, replaced by a kid who looked like he hadn't a care in the world, one his father would be ashamed of. Ever since finding that letter, he'd completely fallen apart.

Movement to his left caught my eye, and I noticed one of the boys trying and failing to subtly brush some suspicious white powder off the edge of the table beside him. They were all out of it.

"Cormac?" I said, gesturing to the mess before me. "Care to explain?"

He stayed mute, and one of his friends opened his mouth to explain but was interrupted when the door at the far end of the room opened and Damien swanned in, a crate of beers in hand. He slammed the beers down onto the table, earning a round of cheers from the lads, only then turning towards me with a look of feigned surprise.

"Oh, sorry Tom, I didn't see you there," he drawled,

flashing me a wide grin. "Care to join us? We're celebrating our new alpha in the making."

I licked my lips, trying to hold back the urge to tear into him and every other guy at the table. "You can celebrate at the next super-moon with the whole pack. He doesn't need some kind of screwed up bachelor's party. This isn't his last night of freedom."

"Why wait?" Damien quipped, snapping open one of the beers.

Every word that came out of his mouth made me want to punch him.

"Grow up," I spat, turning to Cormac then. "That goes for you too."

A chorus of 'ooh's erupted, led by a smirking Damien. I flexed my fingers and only Luke's little hands gripping my leg stopped me walking up to Damien and knocking him out.

"This is pathetic. I expected it from him." I gestured to Damien, my tone cold. "But I expected more from you Cormac. Your father raised you better than this."

He flinched at the sting of my words, his troubled gaze lifting to meet mine. "Just because he raised me to be alpha doesn't mean I'm right for the job. I'm nineteen man, maybe down the line, but—"

"He's just having fun." Damien cut in, circling the table to stand behind Cormac and place a heavy hand on his shoulder. "There's no rule against that. If you expect someone so young to become alpha, you need to cut him some slack. It's a lot of pressure."

I snorted derisively. "Cormac is well able to bear this pressure."

"Is he?" Damien retorted, arching an eyebrow. "We're just looking after him as his friends. Trying to lighten the load."

"You're using him." I growled, gritting my teeth.

Luke tapped my leg, pulling on my jeans to get my attention. "Daddy?"

I looked down, my cheeks heating as he stared up at me with a bewildered expression. I shouldn't have been starting arguments with my son around. Guilt pricked the back of my neck and I sighed, scooping Luke into my arms. "Yes, son?"

"Can we go bed?" he asked with all the innocence in the world shining in his eyes.

"Yes, we can." I ruffled his hair before turning back to the rest of the room, noting how Cormac was swaying in his chair and might have toppled right off if it weren't for Damien's grip on him. "You should all call it a night, if you have any sense."

Damien shook his head, a twisted smile curving his lips. "You might be a father, but you're not ours. We'll do what we want. It's up to the alpha, after all."

I opened my mouth to argue but one look at Luke made me think better of it. "Fine."

With that, I turned on my heel and stalked out of the room. Laughter and jokes had already erupted, instigated by their little ringleader, before I had even closed the door. I slammed it shut with so much force the chandelier in the foyer was still rattling by the time I'd carried Luke to the foot of the stairs.

CHAPTER 10

A few days later, I found Mary in the kitchens, dashing to and from the counter to check items off a ridiculously long list. From my spot in the doorway, I could see her dancing around from one cupboard to the other, a bright smile lighting up her face. There was fresh bread cooling to one side, and she was singing to herself thinking that no one was watching. It was the happiest I'd seen her since her father's death, and it broke my heart to be the one to bring her down. So, instead of doing the right thing and telling her about the death cert, I offered to help her pick up groceries in the city. She chatted animatedly the whole drive there, her bubbly mood making it increasingly harder for me to fit telling her about the death cert into the flow of conversation.

"You've been quiet this morning," she said as we stepped out of the car onto a bustling side street on the north side of the city.

I shrugged, wishing I had the nerve to break her good mood. "I've just got a bit on my mind."

"Well, a problem shared is a problem halved," she quipped, reminding me so much of her mother.

We turned onto one of the main streets lined with shop faces and fell into step beside one another. Mary was clutching a long list written in her tell-tale cursive, whereas I had a list of maybe three items from my father to pick up for the surgery. It was the perfect excuse to spend time with her until I plucked up some courage.

"So, how's Cormac getting on?" I tried to turn the conversation towards home as Mary made a beeline for a fruit & veg store. "Is he nervous about the hunt?"

I didn't need to tell her about his antics the other night. The whole manor had heard her screaming at Cormac when she caught him stumbling home in a state later that night. He would be inducted as our new alpha during the next full moon, which was a supermoon. Legend has it that alphas named during the supermoon were stronger and more powerful. I personally wasn't so sure, but magic doesn't always play by rules that make sense.

Mary shrugged, picking up a bunch of oranges and examining the quality with a keen eye. "He's still sulking. Cormac never wanted to be alpha, he told Dad a hundred times. Now that we know someone wants him dead if he becomes alpha, he wants out."

"I don't blame him, that's a lot of pressure for a kid his age."

"Being alpha isn't a chore, it's an honour. The kid's ungrateful," she said with a derisive snort, dropping the punnet of oranges and moving on to the next store.

I cocked my head to one side, arching an eyebrow. "That's a bit harsh, don't you think?"

"Okay, maybe a little," Mary relented with a sigh, her expression softening. "I just mean, all my life I watched my dad lead, and I was always told the alpha can't be a woman. Losing them is hard enough but having Cormac talking about turning his back on the role just feels like a slap in the face to our family legacy."

"He's nineteen, just a kid really. It's not his fault he's not ready for the pressure. Maybe under better circumstances, he would have grown into the role."

She pursed her lips, unconvinced. "Maybe, but we don't have that luxury anymore."

I reached out, wrapping an arm around her shoulders and pulling her in for a hug. "He'll be okay, he has us to keep an eye on him."

"That's a nice bracelet." She poked the small chain of beads on my left wrist.

I had a few bracelets that I picked up on my travels, but the one Mary was looking at was a string of dark round beads with a cross-shaped pendant. My chest constricted as the memories came flooding back.

The corner of my lips twitched. "It was a birthday present from Laura while she was pregnant with Luke. It was a joke really, but I've worn it every day since."

Mary nodded, returning the hug before pulling away and quickly wiping the corner of her eyes. "I need to order meat for the barbecue."

Every hunt included a big feast for the pack—especially when a new alpha was inducted. Spring may have been around the corner, but seasons didn't function properly in Ireland. Every single one included rain. Not feeling the cold the way humans do had its perks, and year-round barbecues was one of them.

"What's on your list?" Mary snatched the shred of paper from my hand before she even finished the sentence. She scanned the small list, her brow furrowing ever so slightly. "Nightshade?"

"It's on the medical list, not sure why," I explained, unsurprised by her confused reaction.

Nightshade was toxic to werewolves if ingested, similar to how it affects humans but much more potent. Werewolves can heal from nearly everything, not instantly, but it doesn't take a lot for us to heal unless we are impaled or something else prevents our healing abilities. Nightshade is our kryptonite and once ingested, it's lethal. It can only be reversed by pumping the werewolf's stomach or by giving an antidote, and even then, it doesn't always work.

"Tom, I'm not picking up poisons just because they're on the list.

"He might need it for an antidote?"

She shrugged, unconvinced. "There's been an increase in pack fights. I've heard of some gangs using Nightshade on knives in an effort to kill without making it look like a werewolf attack."

"And you didn't think to mention this when we were talking about your father being killed?"

Mary scowled, grabbing me by the elbow and pulling me down one of the side streets for more privacy, making two teenagers up to no good with some spray paint cans scarper.

"I told you, my dad wasn't killed by some gang or a rival pack. If that were the case, he'd have said that in his letter."

I rubbed my face with my palm, that all too familiar headache starting to build. "He didn't say anything about who it was, so why aren't we considering all of the options? What if you're wrong and it is another pack?"

"I know him. The way he wrote that warning, it was someone on the inside," she hissed, slumping against the brick wall lining the narrowed cobbled street. "In the days leading up to his death, my dad was really stressed out and kept making weird comments about not being able to trust his own pack. It made him sound a bit crazy at the time, but now it makes sense. Plus, how else do you explain the weird cover up?"

Now that her good mood had tanked, it seemed like the right time to tell her what I'd found. At least it supported her theory.

"I found the full version of the death cert."

Her hair fell away from her face as she finally lifted her head to look at me. "What?"

"I was giving my father the post and he started acting really weird when he opened one of the envelopes," I explained, hastily tacking on the second part when darkness shadowed her features at my framing her as a thief. "I broke into his desk to see what it was—that thing is like Fort Knox— I didn't think I'd find anything... I was hoping I wouldn't."

"Spit it out," she ordered, her piercing gaze fixed on me.

"I was right."

Mary was silent for a long, dangerous moment.

"They did die from having their hearts ripped out," I said quietly, searching her face for some kind of reaction, but she was still in shock.

"How long ago did you find it?"

"A few days."

I swallowed. For a small girl she could be quite intimidating.

She nodded, disappointment shining in her eyes. "And you didn't think I'd want to know straight away?"

"It's really hard to think that my father had something to do with this."

"And losing my parents isn't hard?" She growled, pushing off the wall and squaring up to me as much as she could. "It's proof that it's an inside job, there's no other reason for your father to hold onto it."

"But we already knew that?"

Mary raised her hand, poking me firmly in the chest, her eyes blazing. "Yes, and now we know your father is either in on the cover up or worse, a suspect."

"We don't know that for sure, he could have just been doing his job," I said, surprised at how quickly I chose to defend him despite the doubts I'd had. "Maybe he thought it would be too traumatic if you or Cormac asked to see it."

"You don't really believe that, do you?"

I sighed, trying to ignore the sense of uncertainty that I just couldn't shake. Ever since the day Mary showed me her findings, I couldn't stop wondering if my father was involved. That's what had me rummaging through his stuff in the first place.

"No, I don't." I raked my hand through my hair and shook my head. "My father wasn't the alpha's biggest fan, but I don't think he's a killer. He had nothing to gain."

She stepped back and rubbed her chin, any anger towards me seeming to have dissipated as her mind raced through the possibilities.

My relief at her not being angry with me anymore did nothing to unsettle the unease in my gut. Every instinct I had was screaming that my father was involved. Mary was right, but it didn't make the pill any easier to swallow. My relationship with my father had always been complicated, but it still hurt to think that the man who raised me was capable of something like this. Killing our alpha was the ultimate betrayal.

"I've caught him talking about the witches, maybe they forced him to do it or something," I said, thinking out loud.

Mary arched an eyebrow. "*The* witches? As in the royals?"

I nodded.

"No. My father was in talks with them and we always paid our dues, why would they want him dead?"

"Your dad wasn't corrupt, maybe they didn't like that?"

"They seemed happy enough that we didn't cause trouble, so I don't think that's it." Mary sighed, kicking a pebble so hard it went skittering across the cobblestones and smashed into a trash can with a bang. "Why would they get involved, especially with your dad? He hates them after what they did to Damien's father."

"Damien was talking to one the other week too."

Mary's frown deepened. "None of this makes any sense. What if they are trying to take control of the pack? Since when are they interested in pack dealings?"

It was time for me to call in the witches too. Niamh, an old friend I came across when intercepting bar fights in my younger days, was a witch that operated under the radar of the royals. She turned up a few times while I was in college to seek help for some strays and owed me a favour or two. Even so, it would cost us.

"I don't know," I said, reaching for my phone and skimming through the contacts until I found Niamh's name. "But I know who might."

CHAPTER 11

Walking down the quays in Dublin City on a Saturday night was weird, especially with everything going on. What was I thinking going on a date? It felt like a lifetime ago that Darren and I would hit the town on weekends. Since having a son, my late nights were usually due to Luke having a tummy bug and not me drinking my own weight in beer. I had to say though, I didn't miss the hangovers.

City lights twinkled under the cover of the night sky. Darkness may have fallen but the city was more alive than ever. Tourists and locals roamed the streets; girls in their high heels and guys in jeans and a shirt. You could tell who had started early by how straight they walked. Rush hour had passed, so the roads were now full of taxis ferrying parties to and from the city centre.

I paused in the middle of the Ha'penny Bridge and looked out across the river, taking in the full view of the buildings and show of lights stretching along the banks. It really was beautiful. London was lovely, but I hadn't realised just how much I had missed my home—my city.

Helena and I had agreed to meet under Clery's clock on

O'Connell Street, cliché, but it felt right. Mary had said that whenever she went for dates, she would take the bus and if her date wasn't waiting for her under the clock, she would just stay on the bus for a few extra stops and meet the girls instead. Cutthroat, but apparently that was a thing. I was out of practice, rusty, and nervous as hell, so I made sure to be early.

There were no pubs here, but the wide, sweeping street was still busy with the last few shoppers catching a taxi home, and friends and couples walking in and out of restaurants at this hour. Across from me, the grey pillars of the GPO towered, the huge building blocking my view of the moon.

Sure enough, I wasn't the only guy waiting under the clock at nine. One guy even had a bunch of flowers, and I found myself wondering if I was doing this all wrong. Darren was the ladies' man, not me. I was settled—widowed.

I had well and truly tied myself in knots by the time I saw a familiar figure winding her way up the street. Helena was in a pair of jeans that hugged her waist and a cropped leather jacket, her auburn curls bouncing as she strode towards me. I noticed her high heels and chuckled under my breath.

"I thought I said casual footwear?" I teased, stepping forwards to hug Helena as she reached me, planting a light kiss on her cheek.

She shrugged, a playful smile tugging at the corners of her lips. "This is casual."

"If you say so." I stuffed my hands in my jean pockets once the embrace ended because I didn't know what else to do with them. "So, should we get going?"

Turning to the right, I placed a light hand at the small of her back to guide her in the direction of our mystery location. She fell into step beside me and I tried not to notice how easy it felt.

"Where are we heading?"

When Helena had put choosing the date location up to

me, I had to admit I'd thought it would be easy. But the more I thought about it, the more I doubted my choices. Eventually, I had to talk Shane into getting some clues from Gráinne which, of course, were as vague as possible.

"Somewhere." I grinned, knowing full well she was responsible for Gráinne's lack of intel.

She nodded, amusement dancing in her eyes. It was the first thing I had noticed. She was so full of life and it was a breath of fresh air. Every sentence had a double meaning, she was keeping me on my toes and for the first time in a while, I felt something in that bruised heart of mine.

We chatted about Gráinne, how she was getting on. All the usual stuff, the news, but nothing about my pack, thankfully. It was all going great until I put my size nines in it and the conversation took a sombre turn.

"How was work?" I asked, just as we were nearing my secret date location.

The briefest of frowns wrinkled her brow. "Not great, I lost a patient."

It was then I realised I didn't know where she worked. I didn't know much about her at all. But I wanted to.

"I know how that feels." I reached out to give her hand a reassuring squeeze—a reflex action that made the blood rush to my cheeks when she didn't let go.

"I'm a nurse," she explained.

I clearly have a type. A while ago, feeling attracted to any woman would have caused an overwhelming surge of guilt. Even joking about the small similarity would have made me feel like an asshole.

"Yeah, I work at my dad's surgery for the moment. When I was in London, I worked in one of the local hospitals."

"With your wife?"

I swallowed, wondering if it had been Shane who told her or if Gráinne had filled her in. I knew I'd have to have this conversation eventually, but I had been hoping it would be at least a few dates in, if we got that far.

"I... Yes, I was married to a doctor in London. We had a son Luke, and she died during childbirth," I explained all in one breath, spitting it out in the only manner I could.

Now it was her turn to squeeze my hand.

"I'm sorry for your loss."

I swallowed the lump rising in my throat.

"You don't care about the kid thing?" The question left my lips before I could register it. I never thought of Luke as baggage and this was just supposed to be a date. The shitshow happening with my pack was baggage, my son was not, but I was aware that it was a lot to ask of someone.

Too soon.

"It is only a first date." She paused, her expression brightening at the thought. "It's a little early for that talk, but yes, I do want kids someday. Your past doesn't bother me, it's what makes you Tom."

All I could manage was a nod, trying not to think about how clammy my hand was getting the whole time.

"Now." She looked up at the bright neon lights hanging above where we had come to a stop. "Can you please tell me why we are at a bowling alley and not a bar?"

I cracked a smile, amazing at how she could transition from something so doom and gloom back to her fun-loving self.

"This is our mystery date location. You asked me to surprise you! Bowling is fun and they serve beer, so it's the best of both worlds." I gestured grandly to the arcade building as if it was a historical treasure, pointing to her shoes with a grin. "Those will have to go though."

We both looked down at her high heels and broke into a fit of laughter.

CHAPTER 12

Bowling turned out to be a really good choice. Despite Helena putting the ball in the gutter half the time, she seemed to be enjoying herself. I was so relaxed around her, all of my worries faded to the back of my mind. She made me feel like my old self again, something I hadn't felt in a long time.

"You really suck at bowling." A low chuckle rumbled in my chest as she rolled a gutter ball.

She spun to face me, shoes squeaking on the shiny wooden floors. "It's hard to focus when I look like a clown."

"Hey, everyone has to wear them, so that's no excuse." I lounged back on a chair, arms spread wide along the backs of the bench, wiggling my feet. My grin only widened as her eyes narrowed. "If you let me put the kiddie rails up, you'd stop striking out."

"Not a chance," she muttered, flopping on a chair beside me. She knocked back a mouthful of beer, folding her arms across her chest, her voice rising a pitch as she whined. "I never used to be this bad."

"So, you were better as a kid?" I teased.

She shot me another dirty look, but it didn't have the effect she desired. Instead it only encouraged my slagging.

"Come on, let's try this again," I suggested, rising to my feet and walking over to the rack. I picked up one of the lighter balls and stopped by the red line, turning to see Helena still sitting in the same spot. "Come over and I'll show you."

She frowned and shook her head. "It's your turn."

"Yes, and I'm sacrificing it to stop you abusing that poor gutter."

"That's your loss." She laughed, walking over to join me and held her hands out for the ball. "Alright, teach me, oh master of the bowling ball alley."

I pulled it away dramatically, faking a wounded look.

She rolled her eyes and grabbed the ball from me, her fingers brushing my chest, and nearly fell over, losing her balance due to the weight of the ball. I caught her by the waist, my hands lingering near her hips long after she had found her feet again. Our eyes locked, and I found myself lost in the moment, studying how the iris of her green eyes had the smallest brown flecks, how right she felt in my arms.

My heart hammered in my chest. I knew what was supposed to come next, but nerves got the better of me. With a nervous cough, I turned Helena to face the bowling alley and tried to guide her positioning.

"So, you put one foot in front of the other, make sure you're grounded and not wobbling or anything," I explained, trying to get my head out of the gutter. "Drop the ball by your side and swing it back and forth to make sure you're happy with the weight of the ball."

The flicker of disappointment in her eyes when I broke the moment was unmistakable and my stomach sank.

You idiot. You've gone and screwed this up now.

"Like this?" She tried to follow my instructions, but her shoulders were tense and bunching together.

I placed a light hand on her shoulders and the other around her wrist to guide the ball. When they said electricity sparked between people in books or movies, I used to think they were just being dramatic, but now I understood it now. I was so conscious of every touch, every movement.

"Almost, you just need to relax," I whispered, gently pressing on her shoulder in indication and entwining my fingers with hers.

Helena nodded, and I noticed the faintest hint of red creeping up her neck. She rolled her shoulders to relax and pulled the bowling ball back, ready to strike.

"Three, two, one..."

I guided her arm as she threw the ball down the alley, watching as it hit the floor and sped towards the pins lined up. It wasn't perfectly straight, but this time it didn't bounce straight into the gutter, shaving off three pins before disappearing.

"I did it!" Helena cheered, throwing her arms around me in an animated hug and planting a kiss on my cheek that made them flush.

I hugged her close to me, breathing in her scent. The embrace was over far too soon for my liking, and I watched as she danced away to grab her beer. She was gorgeous. Every time she smiled, it lit up the room, and her laugh was infectious. Each time we touched, my heart rate skyrocketed. I hadn't felt this way since I was a teenager.

When our game ended, I couldn't hide my disappointment despite winning by a mile. The real prize was getting to spend an evening with Helena. As we walked outside, she wouldn't stop insisting that we needed a rematch, and it made me feel like I was on cloud nine knowing that she wanted to see me again.

"You know, with a bit of practice, I could totally beat you," she joked, still riding on a giddy high.

This time it was me throwing my eyes to the heavens. "Yeah, if you practise twenty-four-seven maybe."

Our hands kept brushing with each step we took down the cobbled street. Those nerves were back, the ones that had surfaced in my teen years whenever I tried the arm around the girl move in the cinema. I finally plucked up the courage to take her hand and entwining our fingers. Helena didn't pull away.

We were walking towards the south side of the city, having decided one more drink was definitely in order, when I noticed a familiar figure lurking in the shadows. Damien was standing in an alleyway, barely visible to a human under the dim streetlight, but I picked up his scent straight away. He was in a tense conversation a blonde-haired witch with angled features. I could sense her magic from across the street.

That alleyway led to one of the underground paranormal bars, a place for dodgy dealings, like a magical black market. I didn't frequent it, but it was the perfect place for a snake like Damien.

From this distance, I could hear snippets of conversation. He was handing over cash, and they were speaking in vague terms about a job. Whatever he was up to, it wasn't good.

Fucking witches.

"What's wrong?" Helena nudged me gently in the side.

I had completely drifted out of our conversation, too busy eavesdropping. It was only when her voice pulled me back that I realised how tightly I was gripping her delicate hand.

"Sorry," I mumbled apologetically, loosening my grasp and rubbing my thumb across the back of her hand. "I thought I saw someone from the pack."

"Another wolf?"

"Yeah, looked like he was up to no good." I exhaled a deep sigh. "But tonight is about you, not my pack."

The little frown that had creased her brow vanished, a soft smile curving her lips. "Right answer."

It felt weird being able to speak openly of my werewolf side. I'd hung out with a few human girls in my early twenties during college, and it had always felt as if I was living a double life. It seemed Gráinne had normalised the strange situation somewhat by telling Helena about the pack.

I didn't want to think about the alpha being murdered, or my father's involvement. I just wanted to enjoy my night.

I decided the bar we had planned to go to felt a bit too close to Damien and his dodgy dealings, so we stopped at an old Irish one in Temple Bar that was werewolf free. Tourists were spilling out of the pubs onto streets, knocking Guinness back like it was water.

"Drink?" I asked Helena as we took a seat in the corner of the bar, striking lucky that we arrived just as another couple was leaving.

She nodded, trying to hand me her purse and rolling her eyes when I refused to let her buy the round. "G&T please."

It took a while to get served and the whole time my brain was buzzing with what I'd seen Damien up to, but I didn't want that. I wasn't going to let it ruin the perfect date night, so I resolved to do as promised and pushed it to the back of my mind. When I arrived back to the table with the drinks and Helena's face lit up upon my return, it made forgetting pack problems a lot easier.

We shared war stories from work, bonding over our jobs. She was the perfect nurse, compassionate and intelligent. As the conversation wore on, I found myself lost in her eyes more than once.

"So, you're an only child?" she asked, stirring the contents of her half-empty gin glass with a straw.

I nodded, not wanting to bring up my screwed-up family dynamic. "Yeah, you?"

"Yep, Gráinne is pretty close to a sister though." She spoke fondly of her friend, her tone laced with concern. "She will be okay, won't she?"

"I promise, me and Darren will help, whether the pack accepts them or not. Cormac is a lovely guy, both him and his father would never see a pack member cast out."

"They found out it's a girl." Her expression sobered when she saw my lack of surprise. "You knew?"

"It's a wolf thing..." I explained, trying not to sound creepy. "From what I've been able to research, because the baby is a girl, it will definitely be a hybrid. That may or may not work in their favour with the pack."

She nodded, but my words did little to ease the worry lines creasing her features. "This is a mess."

I scooted my bar stool closer to Helena's, close enough that our thighs were touching, and reached out to take her hand.

"Please, don't worry about Gráinne. She's with Shane and that makes her family, a part of my pack, and I'll do anything to keep my family safe."

A human could never understand exactly what being part of a pack meant to a wolf, but I needed her to know I would do anything to protect my friends and family.

Helena wore a thoughtful expression as she took in my words, those striking green eyes fixed on mine. "I trust you."

She didn't move her hand away. Instead she leaned closer, and I found myself doing the same, never once breaking eye contact. This time, the nerves didn't get the better of me, and I brushed my lips across hers tentatively. When she didn't pull away, I wrapped an arm around her waist with a confidence I didn't know I possessed and kissed her deeply this time. That electric feeling from earlier soared and my heart thumped erratically in my chest. She felt so right in my arms. I lost myself in her kiss, forgetting about the packed pub around us and my troubles at home. All that mattered was this moment.

CHAPTER 13

When Mary asked me to help her follow up a lead, I was still on such a high from my date that I agreed without even questioning who or what the lead was, happy to go along with whatever she had planned. That had been a mistake. As we pulled up to a police station that morning, I realised that Mary might have actually lost the plot altogether.

"This isn't a good idea," I said, noting how many Gardaí and members of the public were running in and out of the station with umbrellas or ducking under their briefcases.

If Mary went off on one in here, she was going to cause some serious trouble.

She shrugged, turning off the engine and gathering up her handbag. Rain pelted the window, casting shadows on her face. "It'll be fine. Besides, your source hasn't done much."

"Fine?" I echoed her, stunned by her frivolous approach to the situation. "Witches have moles all over the police force, the humans will think you're insane if you start asking weird questions. I thought the plan was to figure out things out on the down low?"

Mary swung to look at me, and it was only then that I

noticed how red her eyes were. "Our plan isn't working, and I'm running out of time. Every day that passes is a day that Cormac is in danger. Someone in our pack wants him dead. It could very well be your father, and I'm not waiting around to find out the hard way."

I chewed my lip, shifting in my seat. "I don't think it was my father, at least not him alone."

"Well, I want answers and I'll be damned if I lose what's left of my family. If what you said is true, Devil only knows what Damien was up to with that witch." Mary growled, getting out of the car and slamming the door behind her.

I groaned, thumping my fists against the dashboard before jumping out and following her across the car park. One of my strides accounted for two of hers, so I caught up quickly, earning a scorching glare for my troubles while almost getting impaled she put up an umbrella. I knew she needed me here, she wouldn't have asked otherwise. So, I pulled my hood up and trudged alongside her, hoping this wouldn't end in tears.

My nose was on high alert as we entered the police station. I caught some old magical scents. There were definitely witches working here and maybe a vampire, but there was no sign of them so far. I silently hoped they were off duty. There were a handful of teenagers sitting in the waiting room, their trainers squeaking on the linoleum floor. Beside them was a guy who looked like he didn't remember his own name with eyes darting in different directions. He was talking to a guard about seeing dragons. A typical Sunday morning most likely, but I can't say I ever spent much time in police stations, so I was no expert.

While I was still figuring out how to approach this, Mary walked straight up to the reception.

"Can I see Garda Brennan, please?" She asked politely, though there was an edge to her tone that suggested this was a formality rather than a request.

The woman on reception nodded, gesturing to a set of double doors to our right. "He's waiting just in there."

Beyond the doors was a long corridor lined with doors, which I guessed were family rooms or interrogation rooms. Beside the nearest door, there was a tall willowy guard waiting for us with his hand out, a genuine smile on his face.

"You must be Mary." He shook her hand with a welcoming smile before turning to me. "Tom, I presume?"

I nodded and returned the handshake, noting how clammy his hands were and how the uniform looked just a bit too big for the lad. He was younger than us, in his early twenties and definitely fresh out of training school.

"Please, come inside so we can talk." He gestured to the nearest room.

Mary walked ahead of me, wearing a pleasant smile that I found unnerving. Something about this felt off.

The room was small, barely fitting a couch and two chairs were placed around a coffee table stacked with magazines. I took a seat on one edge of the couch beside Mary, and the officer shut the door before joining us.

"Cup of tea?" He asked, sitting with his back straight and his hands clasped in his lap.

Mary shook her head, placing her bag down on the floor. "That won't be necessary, I just want to talk about what happened to my parents."

He nodded, sitting back in the chair and rubbing his chin. "This was about a month ago, yes? Car crash in Rockbrook?"

"Yes, that's it, August third." She produced a file which revealed a collection of her newspaper cuttings, and a photocopy of the full death cert I had never actually shown her. "The official line is that they were both impaled on a tree, but that's so unlikely it's pretty much impossible. It would have taken a miracle for a car crash to kill my parents."

I watched the exchange with my mouth hanging open,

wondering how exactly Mary had convinced a Garda to talk to her about this, and why she was talking about her parents like they were superhuman. Then I noticed the way Garda Brennan nodded along, not questioning her comments in the slightest, and the two puncture marks visible on his neck as he leaned in to look at the file.

It all made sense. Mary had gotten a vampire to glamour him into talking to her freely about the accident. Whether she had convinced a friend or hired one, either way it was against the law.

My fingers curled into fists, and I couldn't stop myself from shooting her a dirty look. I understood that she needed answers, but there were rules, and she was crashing right through them without thinking of the consequences, not to mention she was dragging me along for the ride.

Mary took no notice of me, placing a notepad on her knee and sitting perched with her pen at the ready as she grilled the poor guy. "I know it's in your report, but can you please give me an account of the events that night from the moment that you arrived on the scene?"

Garda Brennan nodded, unnaturally relaxed due to the vampire venom paralysing his fight or flight senses. "I was on the night shift and got the call just before eleven. Me and my partner jumped straight in the car and headed out to the location straight away, got there within ten minutes I'd say."

"There's a lot of back roads around that area, how did you find the crash site so quickly?"

Curiosity had gotten the better of me. Just because I was playing along didn't mean I agreed with Mary's underhanded tactics.

"The witness who called was really specific, told us which crossroad to take, and he was still standing beside the wreck with a big flashlight when we arrived," he explained with a shrug, smiling and waiting for the next question.

Mary cut in, sounding like a reporter rather than a concerned daughter. "What did this man look like?"

"Early twenties? He had dark hair and was in a suit. I couldn't see much else in the dark."

"And you didn't get his details?" She pressed, scribbling down every word.

He shrugged, rubbing his chin. "I did. He said his name was Kevin Marks, but when I got back to the station and searched him in our system, the only record we had under that name was a nineteen-year-old. He was a Joe Doe."

"That didn't make you suspicious?" Mary paused her note taking for a moment to glower at the poor guard.

"It was a wreck. A car accident, not a murder," Garda Brennan said, unperturbed by her accusation. Silence followed and he stared into space as he recalled the events of that night. "The car was mangled, the bonnet had imploded and warped around the tree. Both passengers had no pulse. I guess they died on impact, no one could survive that kind of crash."

Mary showed just the slightest hint of emotion as her jaw twitched, and I noticed her writing had deviated from her usual cursive perfection to a bit of a scrawl.

"Is that all you can remember?" I asked, pushing for more details while we had this opportunity, even if it was at war with my morals.

He nodded with a sombre smile, rubbing his palms together. "All I did was take a witness statement from the guy who said he found the car like that, which correlated with the tyre marks on the road. We cordoned off the scene and waited for the paramedics, but the two passengers were pronounced dead on the scene due to blunt force trauma."

I frowned, drumming my fingers against the table. "Nothing was weird? The reports say they were impaled?"

"No, they weren't impaled, but the impact killed them for sure. There was a lot of blood so it was hard to tell, but that's the kind of crash no one walks away from. I'm sorry, I know that's not what you wanted to hear."

Mary found her voice again, having composed herself. "Our family doctor ended up doing the death cert, how did he end up on the scene?"

I should have guessed that question was coming, but it still made me uneasy. I wiped my clammy hands on my thighs and glanced at Mary, guilt nestling in the pit of my stomach. Was it selfish for me to hope that he didn't have that answer, that my father wasn't as involved as we thought, even if it meant Mary wouldn't get the answers she needed?

Any normal Garda would question why she didn't just ask the doctor himself, but under the influence of the vampire venom, Garda Brennan was in a daze and all too happy to help.

"Well, a car pulled up just before the paramedics. It was some fancy silver car, one those loaded businessmen drive. This guy gets out and says he's a doctor, just showed up there by chance." His explanation did little to ease my suspicions. "I thought I'd let him help, just in case I was wrong, and they were alive. Next thing I know, the guy is saying they're close family friends and he's insisting that he stay for the removal and that they get brought back to his place for a post-mortem."

There was no doubt the man in question was my father.

Normally, the pack would intervene before any post-mortem could be done, but that was after we got wind of the situation. Mind links only exist between extremely strong pairings or an alpha and his pack, but there are limitations. There's no psychic link at that distance, no way to know that a pack member or our alpha has died. We pull strings in the background, use connections in the paranormal world. There are protocols in place to stop the human world uncovering more than they're ready for.

"Once the paramedics got involved, they insisted on bringing them back to the hospital first. The doctor guy didn't like that." Garda Brennan shifted in his seat, gazing far away as he recalled the events that followed. "Kicked up such a fuss that my partner had to restrain him until the paramedics could do their thing. Once the ambulance was off towards the hospital, he gave the doctor a dressing down and then let him on the way."

Mary's eyes narrowed and she tapped the lid of her pen against the notepad. "Did you take his name?"

"Yes, it was Fiachra Whelan."

That all too familiar sick feeling surged in my stomach as Mary swung to look at me, her eyes blazing in a silent question.

Do you believe it now?

She closed her refill pad and started packing things into her bag. "That's all we needed, thank you Garda Brennan."

Every muscle in my body felt stiff as I hauled myself to my feet, still struggling to process the confirmation that my father was a murderer. I couldn't run away from this.

"Glad I could help," Garda Brennan said, reaching out to shake Mary's hand with an all too bright smile. "He did have a friend with him though, a woman. I never got her name, but she had blonde hair, good fashion sense and a bad temper. She kept telling him not to get involved. I thought maybe they were on a date or something, and she wasn't happy about it being interrupted. She looked way out of his league though."

I was more confused than ever.

CHAPTER 14

Sitting the seat of a taxi and staring out the window, I found myself wondering how everything had gone so wrong. I loosened my tie and closed my eyes, nodding and giving one-word answers to the poor driver who was just trying to earn a living. I envied him. With so much on my mind, I'd flunked my latest interview. It was a week before the supermoon, over a month had passed, and we had found no proof that my father was guilty. Cormac was still in danger.

I felt like a complete failure. I'd brought my son home to a pack that was falling apart, and my father was at the heart of the damage.

I snapped the visor shut with a snap, the sight of my pathetic reflection only making me feel worse. Instead, I stared out at the bushes and fields flying past in a blur and wished I was heading somewhere else. As we drove up the winding drive, the taxi driver kept commenting on how beautiful the estate was. All I could do was nod.

I gave him a big tip as an apology for my mood and dragged myself out of the car with a heavy sigh. As I trudged up the steps to the manor, there was a loud rumble from the sky followed by the patter of raindrops which quickly mounted to a downpour. I stepped inside just in time and dumped my briefcase, shrugging off my coat.

As I neared the living room, I heard Luke's familiar giggle echoing down the hall, and a small smile tugged at the corner of my lips. The only thing that would make me feel better about my shitty day was the thought of spending the evening with him, just chilling and pretending everything was okay for his sake.

I edged the door open slowly and peeked my head into the room, expecting to see Aoife with Luke on the sofa. Except it was the back of my father's head, his grey-striped badger hair, visible in the flicker of light cast by the television screen.

"Where is Aoife?" I demanded, shoving the door open fully, hard enough that it smacked the wall with a loud bang.

Luke turned to me with wide eyes, his bottom lip trembling for a moment before he recognised me. Fear morphed into a smile and he reached out, doing grabby hands. "Daddy!"

"How did the interview go?" My father asked, swivelling in his seat to look at me, completely ignoring my question.

"Crap," I snapped, walking across the room with large strides to snatch Luke from my father and crushed him to my chest. "Why is Luke with you?"

"Oh, the babysitter?" He shrugged, keeping his voice irritatingly calm. "She's at home. I finished early and offered to mind Luke instead. I am his grandad after all."

"You had no right." I balanced Luke on my hip and nuzzling his cheek much to his delight. "You should have asked me."

"Ask for permission to see my grandson? Well, that's ridiculous."

"Is it?" I challenged, my blood boiling as I thought about

everything Mary and I had uncovered, about what the Garda had said.

My father rose to his feet, brushing down his slacks. "What's so wrong with wanting to get to know my grandson? You're never around."

I bristled. "I was busy trying to get a job."

"Don't lie," he said dryly, boredom seeping into his voice. "You were never a good liar."

"I guess some things aren't hereditary then," I muttered, earning myself a scorching glare.

Mary had asked me not to confront him, to lie low until we had more information, but it was getting harder every day to hide my distaste for him. Seeing the fire in his eyes, knowing I was poking away at the embers of his temper with such ease made it hard to stop. Ever since I'd come home, he acted like I was a burden. He made me feel as if I should have stayed in London, as if I was in his way. My pack was on the edge of falling apart, and it was all because of him.

"Tom," he began, addressing me like one would a child. "I can't help feeling as if you're standing with one foot out the door. The pack needs stability at the moment, and you've done little to nothing about settling in. If you're not with Luke, you're out with Darren acting like a teenager or pandering to Mary. There have been rumours that she thinks her father was killed."

The only people who knew about that letter were me, Mary, and Cormac.

How did he know what we were up to? Did someone tip him off that we were at the police station?

"She's not well," my father said, mistaking my silence as a cue to continue. "I don't want you getting caught up in whatever stories she's chasing."

"You don't think that Luke was murdered? Because I do." I challenged, studying his reactions carefully.

He worked his jaw, his shoulders stiffening. "What are you talking about?"

"You killed the alpha," I said, venom lacing each word. "You killed an innocent man so you could have the pack for yourself."

He rolled his eyes with a dismissive flick of his hand. "I don't want to be alpha, you're talking nonsense. The stress must be getting to you."

Luke poked my cheek, concern furrowing his brow as he looked between the two of us. I set him down on the floor to play with the toy cars scattered on the rug before grabbing my father's arm and pulling him to the far side of the room. Arguing about murder was not something my son needed to hear.

"How do you explain the redacted death cert?" I grit my teeth, my temper simmering. "The one you covered up. And don't lie, I've seen the real one. I know they didn't die in the crash."

My father wrenched his arm away. "How dare you go through my private documents."

"Is that it?" I scoffed, staring at him in disbelief. "You don't even deny it. You're just pissed I went through your stuff? You killed our alpha!"

"Stop it, Tom."

I threw my hands in the air, at a loss for words. "You *murdered* him. A father, our alpha, he never did anything to you!"

"I did not murder him," my father hissed, squaring up to me despite the fact that I had long outgrown him. "I don't need to defend myself. I haven't killed anyone. You need to lower your voice before people start thinking you've lost the plot."

"I know you did, and if you didn't kill him, you at least covered it up. The police said you were on the scene." I growled, towering over my father, the hairs on the back of my neck standing on end. "Don't lie to me."

"The alpha wasn't the saint you or the pack make him out to be," my father snapped, fixing me with an icy stare. "His brother, Patrick, was supposed to be alpha, did you know that? I watched my best friend die at the hand of the witches, and your beloved Luke let that happen. Your mother died because of him!"

I recoiled, the old wounds his words gouged reopening.

"Don't bring mam into this."

He scowled. "Why? Because you don't like hearing the truth about what happened to her? That your beloved alpha let her die, along with Patrick."

I rubbed my face with my palm, rolling my eyes. "He died because he crossed the witches. He stole from them. He got himself into that mess."

The alpha had told me what happened years ago. I remembered asking him about what happened that night because the night Damien's father died, I lost my mother. He explained that his brother got into some dodgy dealings. Drugs, even going so far as to arrange hits—he was in too deep in the darker side of the paranormal world. When Patrick crossed the witches, they came for him, and my mother tried to step in and help because she had a good heart. Too good. She was caught in the crossfire. How my father could blame the alpha for everything that had happened was beyond me. Maybe he had told himself that because he didn't want to blame his best friend for losing his wife, perhaps his warped version of events was easier to live with.

"You need to stop this. Stop sticking your nose where it's not wanted. Stop looking for trouble. Do you hear me?" My father ordered, his tone flat.

I couldn't tell if it was a threat or an order.

With that, he turned on his heel and stalked out of the

room. I was left standing there, my temper bubbling like a volcano ready to explode. He was so sure of himself, too calm. While he didn't deny his involvement, he did deny the murder, leaving me more confused than ever.

I walked over to the couch and sank onto it, watching Luke play with his cars with the innocence only a child could have. He teetered around the place, running a car across my leg, giggling, but I didn't have the energy to smile, my mind too busy racing through everything I knew to try to piece together the truth.

My phone buzzed, and I fumbled around in my pocket for it, the green screen lighting up with a private number. I answered the call and pressed the phone to my ear.

"Tom, hey. Sorry it took so long to get back to you, I ran into a spot of bother that caused some delays," Niamh explained, sounding somewhat out of breath.

I sat up straight, gently holding Luke's little hand to stop him making noise with the car. "Did you find anything?"

It had been so long, I'd given up on hearing anything back from the witch. I'd assumed it was a dead end.

"I wasn't able to get too much working on such a low budget, but I did find out who the witches have been in cahoots with. You're not going to like it."

"It's my father, isn't it?"

The line went silent for a moment before she answered. "No, it's Damien McKenna."

CHAPTER 15

The next full moon came around all too soon. It had been less than a full week since the revelation Damien was behind all this, and we still didn't have a solid plan—or any proof. I wasn't ready to confront my father about it, because I was scared about what revelations that could lead to. On the other hand, I wanted to confront Damien, to make him pay for killing our alpha, the ultimate betrayal. We were running out of time to figure out his next move. Mary knew the moment Cormac was named as alpha, he had a target on his back. We didn't have a big plan, just enough to stop the hunt and buy us time.

The entire pack had gathered in the function room by the time I'd arrived. Luke had kicked up a fuss as I was handing him over to the babysitter. That delay was not part of the plan.

"Tom!"

I turned to see Darren moving through the crowd, two beers in hand.

He pulled me into a quick man-hug and handed me one of the pint glasses. "Nice of you to finally join us."

"Luke was throwing a strop," I said with an apologetic shrug,

Darren laughed, giving me a pat on the back. "I am not looking forwards to that part man."

"You'd need to find a girl first anyway," I teased, taking a long sip of my beer, not that it did much to settle my nerves.

I caught sight of Cormac talking to some of the older pack members and my father. Mary clearly had instructed him on his obligations. She was helping with the drinks, pouring wine and handing out glasses. When she saw me, she gave me a wink, and I followed her gaze to Damien, who was drinking deeply from a wine glass. The knot of tension in my shoulders relaxed just a fraction. Maybe our half-baked last-minute plan would work out.

The delicate mix of wolfsbane and sleeping pills with a hint of nightshade that she concocted should be enough to keep Damien out of action long enough to stop this. Mary working in the kitchens doing catering was the perfect cover.

Once the night had fully taken hold, as if there were some unspoken call, pack members began filtering through the patio doors. I trailed behind with Darren, knocking back what remained of my beer before following the group outside. The trees whispered, the cool spring breeze raising goosebumps on my bare arms.

We walked towards the forest together, the hum of conversation continuing as people chatted, a palpable sense of excitement rising as we approached the forest shrouding the base of the mountain. The pack had settled here many years ago, moving out farther as the city became increasingly built up. It was the perfect spot, with acres stretching into the Dublin mountains, giving us the freedom to run freely while still staying connected to the rest of the world.

As we passed the estate of red-brick houses that was ever

expanding as the pack grew and new generations arrived, Mary fell into step beside us. Her cheeks were flushed, but determination shone in her eyes.

"Did it work?" I asked quietly, turning away from Darren, who was engrossed in conversation with a pack girl he'd had a crush on since he could walk.

She nodded, a wry smile playing on her lips. "Of course, he loves a drink and it was seasonally spiced, who could resist?"

"Good." The word came out hollow despite my attempt to sound positive. I didn't share her enthusiasm.

The full moon above us vanished under the canopy as we broke the tree line, shards of moonlight piercing through until we came to an open clearing, the night sky shining above us. Snowdrops sprayed up in the long grass at the edge of the clearing, marking a turn in the weather. At the centre of the clearing, a delicate arrangement of stones had been erected, a blue fire burning in its centre. This was the gathering place for our monthly hunts and any special rituals, such as initiating a new alpha.

We formed a loose circle around the fire. I stopped beside Darren, but Mary grabbed my forearm, yanking me along with her as she made a beeline around the back of the crowd. She elbowed her way through a few disgruntled members until we were standing either side of Cormac, who shot me a sympathetic look.

I was about to offer some small words of reassurance when my father stepped out into the middle of the circle. Since the alpha's passing, as one of the more senior and respected members of the pack, he had taken up the unofficial position of temporary leader. Although I couldn't deny his willingness to do this only supported Mary's theory of his involvement, I was trying to give him the benefit of the doubt, even if he didn't make it easy.

"Ladies, gents, we are gathered here this evening under the glorious full moon for our monthly hunt," he began, his words carrying across the crowd, which fell silent. His arms were open wide, a sense of authority and confidence filling his voice. "It is a difficult time, one touched by sadness. This is our first real hunt since the loss of our dear alpha, but life must go on."

A soft murmur of agreement travelled through the pack. I chanced a quick glance at Mary, who was staring at my father, her jaw clenched, one hand gripping Cormac's shoulders as if he could disappear at any moment.

My father's expression was more animated than normal, as if he were having a casual chat at the same time as making a speech. It was an odd mix that didn't sit right with me, and I found myself shifting nervously from one foot to the other.

"It is also a time of new beginnings and opportunities. We are the legendary Faolchúnna pack, and we must move forwards as one."

The volume around me jumped as the pack cheered, all eyes fixing on Cormac. He paled, his sister's grip on him probably the only thing stopping the poor lad's legs going to jelly.

Damien caught my eye and shot me a too wide smile. He stood between his mother, Catherine, and his brother, Nick. Something shone in his eyes—excitement—and it made my stomach churn.

"Our alpha was a good man and a strong leader." My father paced in a slow circle around the standing stones. "He will be remembered fondly, but our next leader will be one to remember."

The sense of pride swelling in his voice was unmistakable.

Directly across from us in the circle, Damien straightened up and fixed his shirt collar. Where I was in jeans and a casual T-shirt, he was as formal as a wolf could get away with for pre-hunt drinks. He was hanging on my father's every word, like he knew the speech. As if he knew his cue.

"Can the next in line for alpha of the Faolchúnna pack please step forwards?" My father asked, his words cutting through the noise, the whoops and cheers dying off as a hush fell across the group.

Cormac went rigid beside me. His face was a picture of sheer panic, and I could see small beads of sweat forming on his forehead. There had been countless conversations, formal meetings with head pack members, and encouraging pep talks from Mary. While I had no doubt Cormac wanted to honour his father's legacy, he did not want to be alpha. I wished it could have been different, but we had no choice.

Mary leaned in and cupped her brother's ear, whispering so softly I could only pick up a handful of words. When she was done, she stepped back and gave him a firm pat on the shoulder that was more of a shove. I wasn't quite sure how willing Cormac was as he stumbled forwards into the clearing. He glanced back at his sister, who nodded sharply, and he slowly picked his way to the centre of the stone circle to join my father.

"Cormac McKenna, son of our dear departed Luke McKenna, rightful heir to the position of alpha by blood," my father announced, grabbing Cormac's wrist and raising his arm as if he were a champion in the boxing ring. "Do you wish to lead the renowned Faolchúnna pack under the magic of the full moon?"

He nodded and at a stern prompting glare from my father, cleared his throat. "I would be honoured to lead the Faolchúnna pack."

I was staring resolutely at the ground to keep my temper under control when a chorus of gasps echoed throughout the pack. Even though I knew it was coming, I wasn't prepared for Damien striding into the stone circle join the pair. The smug look on his face as he stopped by father's side made my hackles rise.

"I would like to offer Cormac and the pack another option, one that is fairer for him and in the pack's best interests," Damien declared, his shoulders set, his body language mirroring the confidence of my father's.

I had to reach out to grab the back of Mary's top to stop her lunging at Damien then and there.

Cormac stood beside them, shoulders hunched, looking for all the world like a terrified child. I guess he was.

"Why isn't it working?" I hissed through clenched teeth, forcing her to stay put.

Mary spun and slapped my forearm, forcing me to release my grip on her. "I don't know, it can take a while."

Whispers erupted from the pack on all sides, and from the conversations I did catch, people weren't keen on Damien. *Good.* We needed to rely on their loyalty to Cormac's father.

My father beamed, placing a hand on Damien's shoulder. "My son would like to offer to take on the role as alpha and lead our pack until Cormac feels ready to take over," he said, his booming voice not enough to quiet the crowd this time.

Son? Excuse me?

The crowd erupted into chaos, with people hollering and questions flying from every side.

"Blood alone doesn't guarantee an alpha his place, especially with a boy so young. Please, consider this option." My father turned to the evil leech beside him. "We have to think of the pack."

"Losing Luke was a terrible travesty," Damien began, using words that sounded too grand for him. "But, with every door that closes, another one opens."

"You can't do this!" Mary shrieked, her face a mask of sheer terror.

The look of displeasure that twisted Damien's features gave me the smallest taste of satisfaction.

"Silence!" My father demanded, his voice echoing throughout the forest and gave Damien's shoulder a gentle pat. "Go ahead, son."

Give me strength.

Damien nodded, keeping his cheesy politician smile plastered on his weasel face. "I am a McKenna too, and while I may not have the same strength of blood-right as Cormac, I believe the pack should have a choice. We want an alpha that is young but also has enough experience to deal with pack matters. When he has learned the ropes, I am more than happy to let him take his rightful place."

I struggled to process his words, my fingers balling into clenched fists so tightly my nails bit into my palms. In the shadows cast by the fire, I could see Catherine dabbing her eyes, practically bursting with pride. Nick appeared a hollow shell of himself, staring in horror at the scene unfolding before us.

His little speech had garnered the approval of more pack members than I liked.

Admittedly, he did have a point. Cormac was too young, but Damien wasn't a more worthy replacement. He had no intention of ever letting Cormac take back that role.

I tapped my foot on the ground, unable to hide my disgust as I glared at Damien's smug face. The herbs Mary had slipped in his drink should have kicked in by now. Our plan had failed, we had nothing.

"As a member of the alpha bloodline, albeit not in the direct ascendancy line," Damien continued, absolutely alight and brimming with a confidence that made the contents in my stomach somersault. "I am the closest candidate for the alpha position, as my father was once in line to be alpha."

A rage I didn't know I was capable of nestled in my core,

quickly reaching boiling point as all the pieces fell into place. I didn't need proof. I had struggled to understand why he'd betray our alpha, but it was so obvious, I wanted to hit myself for not noticing in time. There was no accident, only a psychopath on the warpath. He thought his father's right to be alpha was taken from him, that the alpha let him die. He believed the crazy alternate version of events my father dreamed up. He believed it was his right.

"Ancient pack laws decree that where contested, the position of alpha can only be won by a fight to the death. But," my father said, pausing for dramatic effect just to hammer his point home. "If Cormac were to accept my son's gracious offering, there would be no need for this violent, archaic tradition."

Son of a bitch.

Mary sucked in a sharp breath beside me.

We had been so intent on proving what Damien did instead on focusing on what way he was going to play this. Maybe if we had spent time looking up the rules and trying to find a loophole, we would have found a way out of this. There was no way Cormac would win that fight, we knew it, the pack knew it, he knew it.

Damien's eyes shone in the moonlight. He looked like the cat that got the cream, and I could see the cogs turning in his mind as his intricate plan came to fruition. The thought of him leading our pack sent a chill down my spine.

"Do you accept his offer?" My father asked.

Every single pair of eyes was on him, and Cormac shrank under the weight of their stares. His shoulders hunched and his mouth was set in a thin line. He looked to Mary, desperation shining in his eyes and an apology written all over his face. He was backed into a corner.

"Tom lays claim to the position of alpha," Mary declared, her voice coming from behind me.

"What? I—"

The next thing I knew, she planted both hands on my back and shoved me into the middle of the clearing. I stumbled forwards, bewildered and hyper-aware that all eyes were now on me, and I didn't like it one bit.

CHAPTER 16

An ominous breeze whipped through the trees, their swaying shadows cutting through the moonlight illuminating the clearing. The fire burned tall, swelling as if fuelled by the unrest, its flames licking at the inky sky. My mind wandered back to my teenage years, when I had attended my first hunt during my transition phase. I remembered being entranced by the dancing blue flames, the beautiful feeling of magic and nature acting in tandem, a symbol of how it felt when our pack ran together. My father had taken great satisfaction in revealing that the blue fire was nothing more than science, salts, and trickery, but it was our fallen alpha, Cormac's father who had taken a very disappointed younger me aside and demonstrated how the fire never extinguished if starved of air or water. He told me that it symbolised the strength of our pack, burning strong and bright. The flame self-ignited during every full moon and burned until the phase came to a close. There was no deception, just magic.

All at once, the dream stopped, and reality came crashing down.

The gentle hum of whispers ascended into noisy conversation as the pack reacted to the proposal.

My father's face twisted into a furious scowl. "On what grounds do you make this ridiculous request?" he demanded, each word laced with anger and lashing like a whip.

I opened and closed my mouth like a fish gasping for air. This wasn't part of the plan.

"On older grounds than that of blood-right. Ancient rules state that the next in line can nominate any pack member to contest the position of alpha."

Cormac caught my eye and looked away out of guilt. "I nominate Tom Whelan to lead our pack until I am ready to take over. This was the dying wish of my father."

Of course, Mary was never going to risk Cormac's life. She had needed a back-up plan, and it was me.

I looked at my friend, fists clenched in an attempt to stop myself from shaking with a mix of fear and anger.

Her ashen expression and apologetic gaze begging for silent forgiveness did nothing but fan the flames.

"This is a farce. You make a mockery of our traditions." My father whirled on me, his fists clenched as if he might hit me. He pulled up and grabbed me by the shirt instead, as if he were literally trying to shake some sense into me. "Cormac can't just swap with you."

I'd come to terms with my father's cynical tendencies growing up. Never did I imagine I would see him standing in that circle, trying to force the pack to take Damien as their next alpha with blood on his hands. It felt like some sick nightmare, and all I could think about was how I could never raise Luke in a pack like this. His namesake would have been turning in his grave if he had one.

My father shoved me aside and turned to the pack, raising a hand to quiet the crowd once more. Before he achieved silence, the circle parted, and a new cry of surprise echoed through the clearing as a woman strode into view. She was tall, with long platinum blonde curls that fell to her waist. Dressed in a blood-red evening dress and sky-high stilettos, she strode forwards into the centre of the clearing with inhuman balance. The fire lit up her porcelain features, sparkling emerald eyes that foretold of nothing good, and ruby-red lips to finish off her look.

"Larissa." Damien beamed as he rushed forwards to shake her hand, looking as if he might drop to his knees and kiss her feet if given half the chance. "How honoured we are that you have joined us."

Her familiar scent mixed with an overpowering perfume filled my nostrils, and I growled in recognition. She was the same witch I'd caught Damien paying off, and while I didn't recognise her that night, in the firelight I knew who she was on reputation alone. Larissa was a powerful witch, high in rank and devious in nature. She was renowned for having no heart and a penchant for torture. Nothing good would come of her presence. She fit Garda Brennan's description perfectly. The puzzle pieces began falling into place.

"What the fuck is she doing here?" Mary hissed, her eyes narrowing as she inched forwards.

Larissa shook hands with Damien and pointedly ignored Cormac, leaning forwards to whisper briefly in my father's ear —venom no doubt—before turning to address the pack, one manicured hand resting on her hip. "Good evening. I recognise that my presence here may not be well received by many but given the tragic death of your alpha and the difficult months you have endured recently, we witches felt it was only right we send a representative to extend our condolences."

The false apology rolled off her posh tongue with ease. Whether the pack agreed or not, they fell silent.

Mary reached out, grabbing Cormac by the arm and hauling her brother back into line beside her and Darren. She stood angled in front of him, staring at Larissa with an intense hatred, like a Rottweiler on guard.

But Larissa paid her no heed, more interested in putting on a show.

"As you all know, every alpha is endowed with special powers upon their ascendancy," Larissa continued, her hips swaying as she paced in a slow circle while her piercing cat eyes panned over the crowd. Her gaze landed on me and a shudder travelled down my spine. She stopped beside Damien, her lips curving into a smirk. "Damien and Fiachra have kindly asked that I take the honour of bestowing these powers unto the rightful heir, tonight."

"Cormac is the rightful heir," Mary hissed, keeping a firm grip on her brother's arm.

Larissa shrugged, her hungry eyes looking me up and down. "And yet I find he has nominated a worthy specimen."

For a moment, I thought Mary would shove Cormac into the mix again, but something stopped her. Whatever this was, it was planned. We still had no concrete proof of the murder. Whatever plan my father and Damien had concocted, as Cormac was the only true claim to blood right, we needed to keep him safe. Pissing off a notoriously cruel witch was a sure-fire way to kill any chances we had of fixing this mess.

Larissa finally stopped eating me with her eyes and turned to Damien, her expression cooling. "I was never informed the position of alpha would be challenged."

"It's not," my father assured her, waving a dismissive hand in my direction. "Cormac and Tom are mistaken."

Every single pair of eyes were on us, and Cormac shrank under the weight of their stares.

"Are you mistaken?" Larissa asked, her scarlet lips curving into a vicious smirk. "Do you contest the position of alpha, or do you accept Damien as your new leader?"

All I could think about was Luke, his innocent little face,

the sound of his laughter ringing. What kind of father did it make me if I let the pack fall into Damien's bloody hands? I needed to keep him safe, but I couldn't risk him becoming an orphan either.

I worked my throat until the words finally made their way out, my brain still struggling to process what I was agreeing to. "No, I don't accept Damien as our alpha. I accept Cormac's nomination."

She spun in a circle, clapping her hands as she shrieked with glee. "Oh wonderful, I do love a good fight to the death."

My stomach swam at the thought. I told myself that we would find a way out, there's no way I'd let it come to that. We just needed to buy some time.

"This is ridiculous," Damien snapped, rushing towards me with red cheeks and fists balled. "We have waited long enough!"

Larissa threw a lazy hand out and he stopped short, slamming into some kind of invisible wall. "Not tonight. You will honour tradition at the next supermoon."

Before my father or Damien could argue, she clapped and threw her hands to the skies, muttering under her breath in what sounded like gibberish to me. While I couldn't understand the spell, I could feel the surge of power as she drew energy from all around us and channelled it upwards until the clouds began to part to reveal the full moon at its highest point.

Larissa's eyes snapped open and the magic recoiled, snapping back to the source.

"The new alpha will be decided as decreed by tradition. I will return then," Larissa said, her voice echoing throughout the clearing. "Until then, enjoy your hunt."

She turned to face me, long blonde curls whipping with the movement. "Trust your instincts, Tom. Only one gets out alive."

With a callous cackle that made my skin crawl, she dismissed me and walked over to share a brief hushed conversation with Damien and my father. Larissa's magic masked her words, but whatever she said made Damien pale several shades to a nice pasty white.

My shoulders slumped as I exhaled slowly, trying to get my emotions under control. Before I could, Mary walked up to me, nervously twisting her clasped hands.

"I'm so sorry, Tom." Her voice cracked on my name, tears welling in her eyes. "I never planned that. I knew about the loophole, and that Cormac would never win that fight. The thought of him leading the pack.... I couldn't..."

I stared at my friend, struggling to find the words. I understood her reasoning, but the betrayal cut like a knife. My emotions were catapulting back and forth between anger and fear for my son.

Larissa saved me having to find an answer.

"Let the hunt begin!" She announced, clapping her hands as if we were celebrating.

The air quickly became thick with magic seeping from where the witch stood. It washed over the pack, the gentle caress of magic rolling over my skin so at odds with the nightmare unfolding that night.

All around us, the air began to shimmer as the pack shifted into their wolf forms. Damien was one of the first, his body contorting into that of a large wolf with a dark black coat glimmering under the moonlight. Beside me, Cormac's wolf form had a paler coat and was a fraction smaller than Damien, though the difference in muscle mass really showed. He had made the right decision, there was no way he'd have won that fight. Mary was smaller again, her expression sombre as she nuzzled her brother. They trotted off to join the pack taking off through the forest.

Normally, I looked forwards to the hunt, but all I felt was

a steady sense of dread building. I shifted into my wolf form and relished in the feeling of raw power coursing through my veins. My jumbled human thoughts stopped swirling as the wolf in me fought for control.

I sprinted into the dense forest, one of the last to join the hunt. Even the soft turf under my paws and the trees rushing past couldn't calm me. My feet thundered against the forest floor as I quickly made up ground to catch up. Without a clear alpha to lead, everyone was unsure of their place.

In my wolf form, the mix of emotions I felt became something more primal. An intense sense of determination and the need for revenge propelled me forwards. Ahead, Damien pulled up and scampered off to the side, his back arching as he retched. If a wolf could look green, he did. Mary's herbs must finally have kicked in. Anger flashed in his eyes as I raced past. Taking some small solace in his embarrassment, I let my wolf side take over so that my mind could quiet, and lost myself to the wild as I led the pack.

CHAPTER 17

I skipped the post-hunt celebrations. Pacing along the riverbed, I ignored the howls in the distance as I circled back to the manor. The function room was still decorated with Mary's special touch, yet it felt empty and hollow now. I understood that she was trying to protect her brother, but she had put me in the firing line.

I snuck back up to my room and got changed into jeans and a T-shirt, ignoring the nice shirt I'd lain out originally. When I checked my phone, there were two messages. One was from Aoife saying Luke was fast asleep at her house, and the second was from Helena checking in. Nothing from Mary or Cormac, who must have stayed at the hunt. I shot Mary a one-line message to watch Luke if I was back too late. It was the least she could do.

Next thing I knew, I was outside Helena's apartment building in the centre of the city. I parked my car up on the curb and sidestepped a group of drunk college kids as I made my way to the old doorway nestled between two shop windows.

It felt weird turning up unannounced. There was a second

date, and a third, then it just became the norm that I'd come over some nights. Whenever Luke spent time with other kids in the pack, on my days off, spending time with Helena was my escape. Between helping Shane and Gráinne and those nights I got to slip away, I'd fallen for Helena faster than I ever expected.

My finger shook as I hit the buzzer. All around me, the sounds city nightlife rang out—high pitched laughter, the thrum of conversations, shrieks of those enjoying their night. I could even hear the steady base beat echoing from a club several streets away. The city was alive at night, and while I was used to drowning out the noise, it all felt a bit claustrophobic due to the anger still boiling in my veins.

Helena's muffled voice echoed through the speaker, but the line crackled and all I could make out were a few disjointed sounds followed by the tell-tale click telling me to enter.

I nudged the door open and stepped inside, my trainers squeaking on the cement floor as I wound my way up the staircase to her floor. The events of the evening kept swimming in my mind, rotating on a nightmarish loop. Maybe I was a coward for leaving, but I couldn't face an evening of that traitor trying to gain favour.

When I reached Helena's floor, a rectangle of yellow light flooding the landing told me her door was already open. Sure enough, she was standing in the doorway in a cute two-piece pyjama set and bed hair. She still looked half asleep, but one look at me, and concern sparked in her eyes.

"Tom?" She reached out tentatively. "Are you alright? You look like you've seen a ghost."

I snorted, wiping my face with my hand. I wasn't sure if I wanted to scream or cry. Both maybe. "I guess I kind of did."

Her brow furrowed in confusion, but she stepped back and gestured for me to come inside.

The familiar scent of her perfume and the distinct smell

that was Helena filled my nostrils, but it's usual calming effect was muted. The television was quiet in the background, and bedside the couch covered in a snug blanket, a bowl of popcorn sat on the coffee table. In the window at the opposite end of the room, the full moon hung high above the cityscape.

I heard the door click closed behind me and shivered at the sound of Helena's bare feet padding towards me. She wound her arms around my waist, resting her chin between my shoulder blades. "You're roasting."

"The whole werewolves running hot thing isn't exactly a myth, but I'm also pretty pissed off." I sighed when my tone came across flatter than I meant. "Sorry, it's just been a long night."

She unlocked her arms and circled me, tilting my chin up when I kept staring at the floor, forcing me to look into her emerald eyes. "Talk to me, tell me what's happened."

I swallowed hard, trying to find the words. "I think our alpha was murdered by my half-brother—he's not really a brother actually, he's a monster. My father was involved, and mow I'm in line for alpha, as well as Damien, just to keep Cormac safe. We couldn't figure it out on time..."

It was as if she could see my soul. It all came bubbling to the surface, everything I promised I wouldn't tell her. The truth about my pack, about Damien and my father's plans, my life outside of us. The life I never wanted her to be a part of because I couldn't face losing another woman I loved.

She simply nodded, gently rubbing my arm as I spilled my guts. I searched for any signs of fear, but all I saw shining in her eyes was empathy and blazing anger that matched my own.

"I never wanted to tell you any of this," I admitted, rubbing my face with my palm.

Her brow creased ever so slightly as she reached out, wiping a tear from my cheek. "Why?"

"Because it's dangerous. You're a human..."

"What's the point in this if you don't let me in?" She gestured to us, her tone calm despite the bite behind her words. "You can't hide me from that part of you. You're a werewolf, and that's not going to change. If this is going to work, I need honesty."

I opened my mouth to reply but Helena held up her hand to silence me.

"And you need to stop treating me like some China doll that's about to break. I can handle it."

"You *can* break," I whispered, reaching out to cup her jaw, my thumb gently stroking her cheek. "And that's what terrifies me. I don't want you caught in the middle of this."

She leaned in and brushed her lips against mine, and I melted into the kiss. Usually, my troubles faded away, but this was real. It opened old wounds and made me feel in a way I never thought I could again. Only when my magic surged did I pull away.

"Did I do something?" She looked wounded.

I had an idea, and maybe it wasn't one of my best ones, but it felt right. My instincts were calling to me, begging me to change.

I shook my head, flexing my fingers as they tingled. "No, but I need to show you something... I'm going to show you me—the real me."

My head was a mess, and I'd never felt anger like this in my life, but all I wanted amidst the madness was Helena. I needed her.

Before she could argue, I took a few steps back and pulled my shirt over my head. Next to go were my jeans.

She opened her mouth and shut it again. Gone were her witty remarks, blood colouring her cheeks as she stared at my discarded clothes on her living room floor.

Forsaking my boxers, I closed my eyes and reached out to the fire burning in my core. The air around me shimmered as my body began to convulse. Within seconds, my limbs cracked into place and my shape shifted into that of a wolf. It felt surreal to change in the centre of the city, with sirens blaring in the distance. Even in London, we always went on a trip away from the city before changing. The soft fabric of her carpet covered floor felt foreign under the pads of my feet.

Helena's expression went from one of surprise and trepidation, to one of delight once the transformation was complete.

It wasn't the reaction I expected—this should blow a human's mind. There were stories of people going insane when their lover decided to show them a glimpse of the paranormal world. Not every human could cope with their new reality. Gráinne had plenty of time to ease herself into the truth, but Helena had jumped in headfirst without so much as batting an eyelid. And yet here she was, completely unfazed while I stood in her living room in my wolf form.

"This is insane," she said, finally breaking the silence. "You're a wolf."

I cocked my head to one side in a kind of this-isn't-news-you-always-knew-I-was-a-werewolf way.

Helena chuckled and reached out a tentative hand, and I stepped forwards, nuzzling her hand with a soft snort as I exhaled a soft sigh of relief. She buried her hand in my fur, scratching behind my ears like she would a dog. It had the desired effect, and I found myself leaning into her touch. It felt surreal standing before her in my wolf form, and I felt naked in more ways than one, but she made me feel completely at ease.

When it felt right, I licked her hand before backing up a few steps. Reaching out for the energy nestled in my core once more, I willed the transition to reverse. Magic filled the air and within seconds, my bones had snapped back into place, and I was standing in front of her window, showing my ass to anyone looking up from the street.

"Maybe I should've chosen a better spot," I joked, rubbing the back of my neck and grabbing my T-shirt to cover my modesty.

My words spurred Helena into action. She hurried over to close the curtains, her cheeks flushing red.

When she went to rush past me again, I reached out and gently grabbed her wrist with my free hand. My excitement faded as I caught sight of her creased brow. "I'm sorry, maybe I should have waited..."

"No." She shook her head with a sigh. "It's not that, you don't scare me or anything."

I frowned, twirling her to face me, a million potential problems running through my head. "What is it then?"

"You're a werewolf, I'm not."

"That doesn't matter to me," I said, knowing I meant every word.

She took my hand, pressing it to her lips. "I want to be a part of your world, but I know from Gráinne... It's not just about what we want."

I stared into those emerald eyes, the strength and understanding hidden in their depths never failed to amaze me. I really hoped she was wrong. I wanted a quiet life, a happy one, with Luke. If things kept going the way they were, I wanted a life with her too.

As tears brimmed in her eyes, I cupped her cheek and dropped the T-shirt, pulling her body flush against mine. "Whether I'm a werewolf or not, it doesn't change how I feel about you. I won't let my pack dictate my future, that's not the life I want."

She stared up at me, placing her shaking hands on my side. "What if that's not enough? What if we're too different?"

"Normal is boring. Being together is our choice, no one else's," I promised, gently wiping away her tears with my thumb and pressing my lips to hers.

CHAPTER 18

When I rocked up at Helena's, I hadn't planned on staying the night. But sure enough, the stress of the last few months hit me all at once, and I woke in the early hours of the morning, feeling a strange mix between elation and despair. Mary had texted to say Luke stayed with her, but guilt still nestled in my gut. What a mess. Everything felt so out of control. I didn't want to be up for the position of alpha. We stayed up for hours talking about what to do, not to mention what was going to happen to Shane and Gráinne if Damien got control of the pack.

By the time I returned to the manor, the sun rising over the mountains was casting a burnt-orange glow across the skies. It was a breath-taking spot, with rolling fields of wildflowers and the mountain range peeking behind the house. Secluded, the perfect place for a wolf pack. The Faolchúnna legacy. We were once one of the strongest packs in Europe, but now we were heading straight towards being controlled by the witches and Devil only knows what if Damien took control. Luke had always resisted their control, as did the alphas before him. Larissa would garner a lot of sway if she managed to gain control of our pack with Damien in her pocket.

I turned my key in the front door, surprised that someone actually locked it for once, and made my way towards the stairs. I was planning to grab a shower before ringing Mary to see where she was with Luke, when I heard the muted voices and dull buzz of the television coming from the living area.

Taking a detour, I nudged open the door to see Mary curled up on the couch, one hand wrapped around Luke and the other resting on the remote. The steady rise and fall of her chest told me she was out for the count.

Luke was smiling in his sleep, his wolf teddy clutched tight to his chest.

I tried to pull the door closed quietly, but the hinges decided to creak.

Mary stirred and slowly blinked her eyes open, rubbing them with the palm of her hands as she looked up. "Oh hey, I wasn't sure when you'd be back."

"Neither was I," I whispered, tiptoeing over to the couch and perching on the arm.

She sighed, brushing her hair back to reveal dark circles shadowing her eyes. "I'm really sorry, Tom. I couldn't see any other way."

"You could have warned me."

"I hadn't planned on doing that. I thought the herbs would work in time, but I screwed that up." She wrung her hands, staring at the ground as if she wanted to burn a hole in it so it might swallow her up. "I fucked up everything up."

I shook my head, reaching out to stroke Luke's cheek. "I get why you did it, but I'd do anything to protect my family too, and now you're risking Luke having no parents."

"That's not going to happen," she promised, gently removing her arm from around Luke and swivelling to sit upright. "I would never let it come to that."

"I won't fight him."

Mary reached out to place her hand on my arm, fierce determination shining in her eyes. "I will never let Luke lose his father. We will find a way to stop Damien and fix this, you have my word."

"I really hope so." I brushed Luke's hair back, smiling fondly as he mooched around to get comfortable. "If he becomes alpha, the witches control us, and we're just like all of the other packs falling prey to their politics. Your dad would be disgusted. All he ever wanted for the pack was independence and the option to live our lives the way we always have, free to roam the mountains without drama or feuds."

"Damien's father was the one who put a spanner in the works. There were domestics over the years, that's always the way, but Patrick was the one who got in too deep and caused problems."

Every time she said his name, her expression darkened.

"Patrick was an addict with a bad temper and a thirst for trouble," I agreed, tugging at loose threads on the couch. "My father always said it was Alpha's fault, that when the witches came to call in their debt, he should have stopped them. But he was just a kid himself. How was Luke meant to save his older brother when everyone knows the penalty for killing one of the witches is death? He'd bailed Patrick out one too many times."

"He always blamed the alpha for your mam's death, didn't he?" she asked, tilting her head thoughtfully.

I nodded, thinking back to all of the times my father had told me his sordid point of view. "She jumped in to save Patrick's life, the witches snapped her neck without a second thought. My father should have stopped her, but he was more concerned about his friend."

"That's a mess, and Damien thinks it's all the alpha's fault too. This is some sort of sick revenge plot." Mary scowled, her brow furrowing. "My dad was an amazing alpha. Just because Patrick died and lost the chance to be alpha doesn't give Damien some kind of screwed up right to the position. He would be a mess, just like his father."

"I still can't get my head around why he'd work with the witches after what they did," I wondered aloud, slowly rising to my feet. "It makes no sense."

Mary shrugged. "Like father, like son?"

"Maybe he's convinced himself it's the alpha's fault so much he really believes that version of events." I bent down to scoop a very groggy Luke into my arms, tucking his teddy into his little hands. "He's that blind to the truth he'd trust the very ones that pulled his father into the underworld."

"His motives are warped, and they don't help us prove it was him. We need to find something concrete they can't talk their way out of and bring it to the pack." She sat back, slouching into the plush couch with a heavy sigh.

"I better get this little man to bed," I said, scooping up a toy car and the children's book sitting on the coffee table. "There's been enough excitement for one night."

Mary barked a short laugh before covering her mouth, an apologetic smile brightening her tired eyes. "It's like five in the morning. Where did you go?"

"I needed to see Helena."

She didn't push for details, just nodding as her smile widened.

I kissed the top of Luke's head and walked towards the door as she curled up on the couch.

"I'm glad you found her," Mary said, her words catching me off guard for a moment.

I turned my head to look over my shoulder and roll my eyes in full view before heading up to our room.

If only everything else wasn't such a mess.

My world had stopped turning in one sense, yet in another way the days were racing by. Despite my best efforts, Damien was a snake, and I couldn't pin anything on him. I even followed him around for a few days—which is bloody hard when they constantly caught your scent—but I couldn't catch him red-handed. The pack was starting to come around to the idea of him being alpha, especially since he was finding the men more jobs in the law firm. He seemed to pluck money out of thin air for his various projects, peddling dreams of being the best pack ever, as if it were a competition and we were a business, not a family. But the pack members were earning more money, and they still thought of the law firm as Luke's idea, the legacy of our fallen alpha. It was his way to bring us in line with the changes and progression happening in the human world. We needed money to survive properly and connections to sort any mishaps that might arise over the years. It had never been about power or status, the very things Damien was obsessed with.

I was disgusted with my family. Every time I had to make small talk with them made my skin crawl, and I tried to keep

Luke away from them as much as possible with a litany of excuses. Evenings were the only chance I had to do some digging of my own. After work, my father was always busy planning or plotting with Damien, or whatever they did. It gave me valuable time to myself in the surgery.

The days I'd spent sorting out the disorganised mess of an office had really paid off. The filing cabinets were in alphabetical order now, and the different file types were separated. The bookshelves were arranged by topic rather than his previous 'just stuff it wherever' method. When it came to doing research, it was a dream.

With Cormac out of the picture and Damien next in line potentially, our previous plans were in tatters. My new one was to learn as much about hybrids as possible, so that I could help Shane's girlfriend when the time came. As to what happened to them after that and whether he would be allowed live a normal life with her, I had no idea.

I settled down in the office chair with a sigh and just like every day in the last week, I began digging into my research. On the desk beside me was a small stack of medical journals on hybrids in mammals that I had pulled, and then some of my father's handwritten notebooks. The man was a disgrace, but that didn't mean his medical knowledge couldn't come in handy.

The fax machine started bleeping, and I jumped up, running over to the machine and watching with the excitement of a kid on Christmas Eve for the message to print.

During my time in London, I had only met one hybrid. A young woman in her early twenties, who came in after getting a beating on the streets from a rival pack. While her pack accepted her, others were not so forwards thinking.

While I had no problem with hybrids, many did. Werewolves were an old breed, entrenched in tradition. The advancement of the human world in recent years had accelerated at an unprecedented rate, and with cameras more prevalent, it was becoming harder to hide our existence. While they were weaker in terms of strength, hybrids weren't bound by the moon, a distinct advantage when it came to holding territory. Hybrids were different, they had always been around, but out-breeding was rare and the baby was usually killed. Now it was becoming more common, due the fear of change and letting humans into their packs, werewolves were struggling to adjust.

At the time, I was shadowing another doctor—a werewolf —who had seen hybrids before in one of the Scottish packs. He had done some research himself, just basic questions and looking into historic references since we couldn't test the girl's blood. There were no records of any male hybrids. When mating with humans, it seemed that no matter what the combination, hybrids could only be female.

When we got back from meeting Shane, I had phoned him up in London straight away and explained the situation. He agreed to fax me over what research he had written up on the promise I didn't let anyone else get their hands on it. That part was easy—I could count the amount of people I could trust on one hand these days.

I cast a quick glance over each sheet as it printed and couldn't stop myself from grinning. This was exactly what we needed. It would have taken me months to gather everything, and we didn't have that kind of time. At least with this, Shane and Gráinne could make an informed choice about their future.

The floorboards outside creaked, and I froze.

"What's this?"

I turned to see Damien standing in the doorway, staring intently at the papers in my hand.

"It's nothing." I growled, folding up the papers. "Have you ever heard of knocking?"

I cursed myself inwardly, knowing I needed to up my guard properly. I should have smelled him coming. Living in the manor had its disadvantages. Because he and my father were inseparable, the office stank of Damien, which made it easier for him to sneak up on me.

"It doesn't look like nothing." His playful tone had a dangerous edge.

"It's just feedback on a job application to one of the hospitals. Don't you have somewhere to be?" I asked, my tone blunt.

He shrugged, his gaze flickering to the stack of papers I'd printed. "Not really."

Before I could stuff them into my bag, Damien was next to me, his bony fingers closing around the papers. His grip was strong, but mine was stronger and I refused to yield. Like a petulant child, he tore a thick strip of one of the papers from my hand.

"Give it back." A low growl rumbled in my chest and I quickly stuffed the remaining papers in my bag.

"It appears that hybrid inheritance is related to the X-Chromosome." Damien's mouth twisted in repulsion as he read the passage aloud, his tone dripping with disgust. "Why are you reading about hybrid scum?"

I snapped my laptop shut. "None of your business."

"Oh dear," he said, his face lighting up with some sick kind of amusement. "Don't tell me you had a rebound? Is little Luke getting a little mongrel runt for a sibling? Laura would be disgusted."

My control snapped at the mention of her name, and I launched myself at Damien, slamming him up against the office wall. I had him pinned by his shirt collar, claws extending from my fingertips and ripping the material.

"Touch a nerve, did I?" he sneered, gripping my wrists

tightly as he tried to pry me off. "Mongrels will never belong here."

He kicked out aimlessly and I pinned his leg with my knee. Damien had never taken much interest in fighting, and I was the one who taught him most of his moves.

"You never did learn to fight," I spat, wrapping my hand around his throat.

I caught the tiniest flicker of fear in his eyes, but it vanished as quickly as it surfaced.

Tightening my grip, I shoved him back against the wall each time he tried to escape my hold. "You really have become a monster. All those years I defended you when people said you were trouble, and now look at you."

Damien dug his claws into my wrist as a sick smile curved his lips, amusement sparking in his eyes. "Exactly. Look at me, I'm going to be your alpha."

"Over my dead body,"

"That's the plan, unless you back down."

My lips curled back as I snarled and pulled my fist back, ready to beat the living daylights out of him, all of the pent-up anger and frustration I'd been bottling up coming to a head.

He killed our alpha.

Rough hands gripped my shoulders and pulled me off him. I screeched like a feral animal and swung an elbow back into whoever had grabbed me, lunging at Damien once more but their grip on me didn't falter. The coward knew he had pushed my buttons too far and stared at me wide-eyed before bolting out the door.

I swung around to see Darren, breathing heavily and nursing his side where I'd clipped him.

"What were you thinking man?" He winced, slumping into the desk chair. "You can't attack him. I don't agree with it, but with the witches involved, you can't take him out before the real fight. I thought you didn't want any of this, why not just wait until Cormac is ready?"

"As if he'll ever give up the position," I spat, bending down to pick up the piece of paper Damien had dropped in his hurry to leave and placing it in my bag with the rest.

"What do you mean?"

"Nothing." I shook my head, perching on the edge of the desk with a deep sigh. The red mist slowly lifted, and my claws retracted. "Forget I said anything."

CHAPTER 20

Following my not-so-little outburst, Darren dragged me out of the manor. I couldn't get a word of protest in before Darren was already on the phone to Aoife asking her to babysit for longer. He wouldn't take no for an answer, bundling me into his car and driving all the way into the city without speaking a word. When he pulled the car up in a dingy alley off one of the many winding side streets, I knew what he was up to.

"Drinks? You really think a shot of whiskey is gonna fix this?" I asked, the leather of Darren's racer seats squeaking as I swivelled to glare at him.

He shrugged, humour flashing in his eyes. "You won't tell me why you were trying to knock seven shades out of your competition for alpha besides the obvious, so I need to loosen your tongue somehow."

Tension tugged at my shoulder blades as I shuddered. Hearing Darren refer to that rat and the position of alpha in one breath made my temperature climb again.

Darren hopped out of the car, the gentle care with which he closed the car door was at odds with the force behind his steps as he strode down the alley, disappearing into the shadows. He didn't wait for me to follow.

As much as he was a joker, he was clearly pissed off with me. We were like brothers, thick as thieves—we didn't keep secrets. After all these years, we had fallen back into our roles with ease. Except, this time, I'd lied to him.

With a reluctant sigh, I slammed the door shut behind me and followed Darren into the alley. The stench of trash cans and the muted thrum of a rat's heartbeat layered on top of the general city din, adding to my discomfort. I remembered coming to the city at night after shifting for the first time, how the sirens and the beat of the bass from clubs had made me feel like my head might explode. Being able to zero in on what I wanted to hear and reducing the rest to background noise was a skill that required practice, but it was worthwhile. Had I come from some quiet little village when I moved to London, I would've been knocked for six. Dublin was tiny in comparison, but my little city gave me a good steppingstone.

By the time I caught up with Darren, he was stubbing out a cigarette on the cobblestone with the heel of his shoe. Tall walls made of mismatched stone lined the alleyway, the walls covered with worn old posters peeling away. Darren stood in front of an old steel door reddened with rust. The handle looked like it would crumble if touched.

"What have I told you about mistreating Maria?" Darren glanced up, his lips thinning.

I'd never met a man who loved his car more. I didn't even try to plead my innocence—any anger taken out on that car was a personal slight on him.

Darren turned and rapped his knuckles against the rusty metal door. The hollow noise of the raps echoed throughout the alleyway, bouncing off the walls. Then the magic began.

The air surrounding us shimmered and the door groaned as it contorted, the alley quickly charging with magic. The handle pulsed and warped as the door transformed into a large oak door, complete with a new gold handle and trimmings. It swung open without command to reveal two tall men with broad shoulders dressed in tailored suits.

Darren stepped through the doorway, and I followed, exhaling as a rush of warmth washed over me.

"Good to see you, Alec," I said, giving the man to my right a slight nod as we walked past.

The Dark Night was a popular bar in Dublin that catered for a whole range of paranormal clientele. Small dancing flames hovering like ceiling lights that lit our way to another set of doors lined the red-carpeted corridor, which opened into a large room filled with tables in the centre and a long bar stretching the full length of the wall on the left. Snugs with small couches lining the other walls were filled with patrons laughing and drinking, and a large spiral staircase nestled in one corner wound its way up to a balcony. Wooden beams supported a high ceiling decorated with coloured panes of glass, reminiscent of a church. The vampires that owned this bar loved to revamp it every few years. The latest look was a bit of a pun.

Darren made a beeline for the bar and a pretty barmaid, while I meandered through the seats until I found an empty table.

I reached out and tapped the shoulder of a woman in the nearest group. "Is anyone using this?"

She turned, her set of striking blue eyes zeroing in on me. "Sorry?"

"The stool, can I borrow it?" I motioned to the stool beside me and doing my best to ignore the melodic tone of her voice.

Cocking her head to one side, the woman studied me for a long moment, as if toying with potential prey. Eventually, she broke the spell and her lips curved into a friendly smile. "Of course."

"Thanks." I muttered under my breath about sirens as I pushed the stool back over to my chosen table.

Like clockwork, Darren appeared with two pints of beer in hand.

"What's got your knickers in a twist now?" he asked, smirking as he followed my line of sight and spotted the siren. "Aw come on, they're harmless. It's all a bit of craic, something you've been lacking lately."

I just shook my head and sank onto the stool, pulling one beer over to my side of the table. "I do have fun."

Darren arched an eyebrow, taking the seat opposite me. His playful side had returned now, any harm I'd caused dear Maria long forgotten. His good nature never let him harbour a grudge for long. Maybe that was why we were such good friends—I did enough brooding for both of us.

"You seem to have calmed down a bit," Darren said, knocking back a mouthful of beer. "Sirens aside."

I shrugged, playing with an innocent beer mat. "I'm fine."

"Uh-huh, because throwing punches is fine. Not to mention running for alpha without even telling your best mate." He snatched the torn-up beer mat from my grasp so I was forced to look at him. "I know Damien is an annoying little shit, but are you going to tell me what's really going on?"

"That's no way to talk about our esteemed alpha," I quipped.

"Cut the crap." Darren gave me a deadpan look. "He's not the alpha yet."

I sipped my beer, an excuse not to have to answer.

"You were about to knock him out," he argued with a chuckle, sighing fondly at the memory. "Just tell me what's going on."

"Ugh, this is such a mess." I groaned, rubbing my temples

before placing my palms on the table and taking a deep breath, followed by a long exhale. "It all started when I came home from London and the alpha died. Mary found a letter from her father warning that he knew he might die, and that Cormac was in danger. We went digging, talked to the police and everything."

Darren stared at me, eyes wide and his mouth hanging open.

"It started looking like my father was responsible for the alpha's death," I said, the words tasting foul on my tongue.

"No way." Darren's grip on his pint glass tightened. "I mean, it's no secret your dad wasn't his biggest fan, but Fiachra is harmless."

I didn't approve of my father's involvement, and our relationship was dead and buried as far as I was concerned. Despite this, I couldn't help wondering how much he was responsible for and how much of the plan was Damien's warped idea. Whether my father was blackmailed into helping or helped of his own volition, he was a disgrace to the pack. Regardless, Damien was a monster of his creation.

"I found it hard to believe at the time too." I took a slow sip of my drink to ease the admission. "It didn't make sense. But then Damien put his name forwards for the position of alpha during the hunt, and everything became clear."

Darren blinked slowly, putting the facts together and quickly joining the dots to come to the same conclusion Mary and I had been living with for too long.

"Damien did it..." he whispered, leaning in closer, the faintest hint of tears making his eyes glassy. "Damien killed our alpha. Is this all because of what happened to his dad way back?"

I nodded solemnly, watching the realisation wash over him. Darren had never been one to show emotions, always coming across as cool and carefree, but I knew he was a big softie at heart. Losing an alpha, our leader, hurt in a way no human could fathom. It was like an innate magical bond had been broken, and it brought with it an avalanche of emotions. Losing him once was one thing, finding out he was murdered brought it all back tenfold.

"I'm going to kill him." Darren growled, knocking his stool over as he leaped to his feet.

Of course, he jumped straight to the anger stage, bringing us to the same page.

I reached out and grabbed his arm, using my free hand to right his stool, apologising to the table beside us as I firmly shoved Darren back onto the seat.

"I get it, I do. Now you see why I wanted to deck him." I dropped my voice low to avoid drawing any more attention.

Damien didn't go to the Dark Night. It wasn't his scene as far as I knew, but if he had the witches on his side, he had ears everywhere.

"Why didn't you tell me this sooner?" Darren demanded, grabbing his beer and knocking several mouthfuls back before slamming it down with so much force the glass cracked and the cool liquid pooled on the table. He stared at the mess and rubbed his face with the back of his hand, his voice breaking. "I could have helped."

I gave his shoulder a heavy pat and started mopping up the mess he'd made with a napkin. "I was trying to keep you safe. We weren't sure what we were dealing with."

"And now?"

"Now you need to know because Damien hates hybrids and that's what we were fighting about. He will never accept Shane or the baby," I explained, tossing the damp ball of napkins into the half-broken glass as I met his steady gaze.

Darren sighed, his jaw twitching. "I don't need protection."

"No, but that baby does."

My phone started buzzing, sending vibrations through the table and scattering more glass. I was going to ignore it until Helena's name flashed up on the screen.

"Just answer it, lover boy." Darren waved his hand in dismissal.

I picked up the phone and clicked the flashing green phone symbol, pressing it to my ear. "Helena? What's up?"

All I could hear on the other end was a scream, followed by Helena's voice coming in and out, but she was speaking so fast each word blurred into the next.

"Helena?" I frowned, pressing the phone firmly to my ear and covering my other ear with my hand to drown out the background noise of the bar. "What's wrong?"

Darren sat up straighter in his chair, his brow furrowing as he watched the exchange.

"Tom, you need to get here. There's an ambulance on its way," Helena said breathlessly, panic clear in her voice.

"Ambulance? What's happened?" I asked, jumping to my feet and grabbing my jacket before motioning for a concerned Darren to follow.

Helena's voice became distant as she tried to calm someone in the background before coming back on the line. "It's Gráinne. I think she's in labour."

CHAPTER 21

By the time we were halfway to Helena's, we were told to reroute to the hospital instead. I managed the phone, contacting Shane and making sure he would meet us there, fielding texts from the girls while Darren hit the gas and broke several traffic laws, including losing a Garda car tailing us for speeding, to get us to the hospital in record time. We dumped the car outside, Darren taking up two spaces with his shoddy parking, and ran full speed for the reception.

As we passed an elderly woman having a smoke outside the entrance, something occurred to me. We couldn't go sprinting into a human hospital. As far as they were concerned, this was a normal baby.

"Slow down!" I grabbed Darren by the back of his shirt when he ignored me and shoved through the front doors, pulling him back. "We can't go barging in there."

Darren spun to face me, but where I expected to see his eyes flashing silver as he fought his temper, there was concern.

"Act normal. It'll all be ok," I promised, giving his back a gentle pat.

The hospital foyer was pristine white with a reception and

a handful of shops, and a busy café. Staff dashed from one area to the other, while visitors milled around. Darren looked around lost, so I strode past and headed straight for the receptionist desk, a friendly smile plastered on my face.

"We're looking for a Gráinne," I explained, unperturbed as the receptionist stared down her spectacles at me. "She would have been admitted through ER, around thirty-two weeks pregnant with contractions, small, dark hair, probably had a guy who looked terrified with h—"

The receptionist held up a hand to silence me, and I promptly closed my mouth. Darren stood behind me, dancing on the spot and weaving like a horse ready to bolt.

After what seemed like endless clicking by the receptionist, I spotted a woman walking across the foyer towards me, clipboard in hand. "Tom!"

I did a double take, realising it was one of the girls I went to university with. "Bríana! It's so great to see you."

"Are you okay?" she asked, her broad smile faltering as she looked between the two of us.

Darren was prancing on the spot, desperately trying to get Shane on the phone. It was one of the first times I'd seen him too panicked to check out a girl.

"It's great to see you. My best friend's brother's fiancé is in labour, but she's two months premature, so we need to get to her," I explained, giving Bríana a warm hug, cringing when I realised I sounded like an American laying claim to their non-existent Irish ancestry. "She came in through A&E."

"Small? Black hair?" she asked, tabbing her pen against the clipboard before her face lit up. "I remember her, she's still in cubicles. Follow me."

With that, Bríana spun on her heel and cut through the line for the reception which had formed behind us. I grabbed Darren by the wrist and pulled him along. We followed her down a maze of corridors until we found the A&E, directions the receptionist could have easily given us. I focused on making casual conversation while Darren wound himself up further with each step we took.

"What brings you back here again?" Bríana asked, quickly checking her pager as we walked.

"I decided to move back home with Luke." My palms were growing clammy as my heart rate climbed. The familiar scent of antiseptic filled my nostrils, coupled with the constant bleep of heart rate monitors, had memories I'd rather leave buried resurfacing.

"Ah yes, he's the image of you. I was sorry to hear about Laura. It feels so weird when you find out these things over social media, of all things," she said with a sigh, quickly giving me a gentle pat on the shoulder when I fell silent. "That wasn't a dig, by the way. Keeping in touch is hard, especially after what you've been through."

I nodded, not quite sure I could form the right words.

Bríana led us through the ward, past the odd emergency mix of clientele ranging from drunks to the elderly with a few broken bones, children screaming bloody murder, and parents fretting. She stopped by the cubical at the quieter end and pulled back the curtain.

"Here we are."

Gráinne was lying in the hospital bed, a thin sheen of sweat beading on her forehead, while Shane and Helena stood on either side of her bed. Shane looked queasy with nerves, rushing over to give his brother a big bear hug. Helena's brow was creased with concern, her emerald eyes glassy as she looked up and gave me the smallest of smiles.

But one glimpse of Gráinne told me she wasn't in labour. She looked worried, scared, but she most definitely wasn't experiencing contractions.

"What's going on? I thought she was in labour?" Darren asked, quickly coming to the same conclusion as me.

"She was," Helena explained, giving her best friend's hand a reassuring squeeze. "At least we thought she was."

"I'm no expert, but I'm pretty sure you can't just magically *stop* labour," Darren said dryly, using air quotes to hammer his point home.

"Oi! Cop on Darren," I snapped, peering at Gráinne's chart over Bríana's shoulder. "She was admitted with contractions, but if they've stopped, they're Braxton Hicks."

Darren was ready with another witty comeback, but Shane gave his brother a warning look. Stepping up to the plate, he placed a gentle hand on his fiancé's arm. "What does that mean?"

"It means she's not in labour, not yet anyway." Bríana took the clipboard from me and cleared her throat. "Braxton are kind of like a trial run, they're basically false labour pains."

I stepped back and let her take over the explanation as it turned out she was the doctor treating Gráinne since her admission. All scans were clear and that was the main thing. It's a small world and Ireland's even smaller. There's always someone in common around the corner.

"They don't feel fake," Gráinne mumbled, bracing her elbows to raise herself up and wriggling back a bit in the bed so she could sit up.

"I agree, they are really common and completely normal though. You've nothing to worry about." Bríana chuckled.

The group of us shared a look and bit our tongues, knowing full well we had so much to worry about that a normal human doctor could never fully understand.

"If you'll excuse me, I'm going to process your discharge papers so you can get home and put your feet up." With that, Bríana turned and walked out of the cubicle. Before she pulled the curtain closed, she turned to me once more. "I know you're probably still getting settled in or have something else sorted, but there's a vacancy here if you fancy it. I can recommend you to the clinical lead."

"I applied but didn't hear anything back," I said, feeling the familiar tension of feeling like a failure creeping up the back of my neck.

She frowned. "I was the one who went through the applications, I'd definitely have recognised your name."

Realisation bitch slapped me full force in the face. *He's been controlling every fucking thing.*

"Must be a mistake." I said, trying to keep my tone even as my temper simmered under the surface.

I'd been wondering why I was getting nowhere, especially when my father said he was recommending me, but he was in the perfect position to block any jobs I wanted, and I had no doubt Damien was the one orchestrating the sabotage. I was overqualified for half of the jobs I'd applied for. Years ago, he'd pushed me to go to London because he wanted me out of the way, now he was trying to stop me settling down because he didn't want me around. How long had he been manipulating everything to get his way?

"I'll happily give you my backing," Bríana said, giving me a gentle pat on the arm that brought me back to the moment. "It would be nice to have a familiar face on the team."

"That would be amazing, thank you so much."

She flashed me a smile before closing the curtain, her heels clicking on the linoleum as she walked away.

My elation was short-lived. When I turned back to the group, all of them wore the same worried expression.

Helena shuffled over to my side, planting a gentle kiss on my cheek and linking her arm with mine interlacing our fingers. She felt warmer than usual, and I could hear her heart racing. She was so strong, she'd never let her fear show, but I knew Gráinne was like a sister to her. That's why her and

Darren always clashed—they were both stubborn and overprotective.

I swallowed the lump forming in my throat as I watched Shane comfort his fiancé. They were so young, and what should be one of the happiest times of their lives was tainted with pressure and fear. We were running out of time, and they didn't even know the half of it. Damien would never accept the baby. He was a monster, and I had no idea how far he would go to protect his screwed-up vision for the pack. They would never be safe with him around.

Darren gave me a curt nod of understanding.

He rolled his shoulders and heaved a heavy sigh before turning to Shane and Gráinne. "I need to tell you something."

CHAPTER 22

Being stuck in a room full of screaming kids, toddlers throwing tantrums, and babies wailing was not my idea of a perfect Friday night, but this was my life now as a dad. Gone were the weekend blowouts, replaced by trips to zoos or food chain restaurants. Instead of breaking up bar fights or flirting the night away, I was pleading with my son to stop throwing chicken nuggets at the poor woman sat at the next table over, promising milkshakes and toy cars, anything for a hyperactive Luke to sit still.

"Either behave, or we're going back home." I caught Luke's little fist just in time to stop him launching another piece of chicken into the air. "Big boys don't play with their food."

"But wolves do. You play with deer," Luke huffed, his bottom lip sticking out.

I sighed, dipping the chicken nugget into some ketchup and taking a bite myself. "I don't actually, I let the rest of them kill the deer."

The woman Luke had targeted glanced up from her meal, eyes wide and staring as if I was a lunatic. When I caught her eye, she quickly dropped her gaze and started chatting to her child instead.

"No talking about wolves outside of the house," I murmured, giving Luke reproachful tap on the nose. "Remember?"

He shrugged, grinning widely as he stuffed another fry in his mouth.

In London, if you were talking about wolves, people assumed you were working on a movie set. If someone talked about wolves or witches in Dublin, the average human presumed they'd lost the plot. Maybe I had.

As Luke rummaged around in the bag of nuggets, I noticed a small bracelet on his wrist.

"What's this?" I asked, reaching out to examine the bracelet.

He slapped my hand and whined, tugging it free so he could nibble on more fries.

I frowned, ignoring his tantrums as the whine became a squeal, leaning in to examine the delicate band. As my fingers brushed the surface, pain shot through my hand and Luke screamed. I recoiled in horror before gathering him into my arms, holding him tight to my chest.

Silver.

Who would give him this? Silver wasn't a myth; it really does hurt werewolves. It sears our skin, and while a normal bullet to the heart would work if it hit the right spot, silver would seal the deal. It shouldn't have hurt Luke until he turned, but I could feel the tell-tale presence of magic infused in the bracelet. Whatever the spell was, each time it was touched it projected the pain silver causes on Luke too.

"Luke," I said, trying to coax his attention back to me with a nugget, pointing at the offending item on his wrist. "Who gave you this?"

He snatched the nugget from my hand, tears streaming down his face as he munched on it.

No matter how many times I asked him, I couldn't get a straight answer. I didn't know what I expected from a toddler. Conscious of the many eyes on us and the mother to my right muttering I shouldn't be allowed have a child, I scooped up Luke and his little bag of toys, careful to avoid activating the bracelet again, and strode out of the fast food chain.

The whole ride home, all I could think about was the bracelet and the look of horror on Luke's face when I touched it. I hated my father, but I needed to tell him about the bracelet. I didn't trust him, but he loved his grandson. He was the one who would know how to get it off in the most painless way. Magical objects were above my skill set. I slammed my fists on the steering wheel and cursed myself for ever bringing him home, for letting him get hurt. Laura would have been horrified had she still been around to see the mess I made.

Who would do this to an innocent kid?

I wasn't sure why I even asked myself the question—I knew the answer. The man who killed our alpha was more than capable of hurting a child. Damien was a psychopath.

By the time we reached the manor, the sun hung low in the sky, colouring it a deep orange while setting over the mountain peaks. I found myself wishing I could do a U-turn and take Luke somewhere else.

A classy, executive black limo passed me on the driveway, its look alone highlighting how out of place it was here.

I pulled up in my usual spot before cutting the engine and slouching in my seat. Beside me, Luke looked up from his toy and stared at me with his mother's hazel eyes, a wide grin stretched across his face. He was the one thing keeping me sane.

"Come on little man." I carefully reached across to

unbuckle him from his car seat. "It's getting close to your bath time."

Luke squealed in protest at the word bath, bopping me in the head with his toy car. "No."

I chuckled and shook my head, hoisting him onto my lap. Immediately, Luke swivelled and started toying with the steering wheel. When he started bashing the car horn with his little fist, I exhaled a reluctant sigh, wrangling him into my arms and out of the car. I slung his bag of tricks over my shoulder and tapped the car door shut with my foot.

Wasting no time, I dropped his bag inside the door and jogged straight up the stairs towards my father's room. I rapped on the door, but I couldn't hear him. On my way downstairs, I heard strange voices drifting towards me.

I hovered in the shadows on the landing, my hands resting lightly on the banister rail as I looked over the balcony into the foyer. Damien stood at the door, suited up with his politician's smile plastered on his face as he gave his guests the grand tour. My father was by his side, and I was beginning to think he was more of a puppet master than a dutiful father figure.

"What the hell is he up to?" I muttered under my breath, craning my neck to get a clearer view of their faces.

The men he'd invited over were vampires—I clocked the lack of a heartbeat from my hiding spot. Why he was inviting vampires into pack territory, I had no idea. I was fine with vampires, but then, I was far more progressive than most of the pack. Damien thought werewolves were the superior race, so to see him shaking hands with a vampire and inviting them to dinner meant he was definitely up to something.

Isn't he always?

"Lars," Damien crooned, full of enthusiasm as he shook the last man's bony hand. "I really appreciate you accepting my invitation."

I cast my senses out fully and sniffed, my stomach sinking

when I realised I recognised this one by name and reputation alone. Lars was an elder in one of the older vampire covens in the city, greed and brutality his trademark. He wasn't a man I'd ever invite into my home, but I guess he and Damien had a lot in common.

Now seemed like the perfect time to interrupt this little meeting before they could build any form of an alliance or cook up some nasty plan together. I rushed down the stairs, making as much noise as possible and tore through the hall towards Damien, roaring his name at the top of my lungs. I didn't care who heard me. In fact, I think an audience was exactly what I wanted when I got my hands on that weasel's throat and showed them all what kind of murderous asshole he was.

He saw me coming and quickly ushered his guests into the dining room, locking the door behind them.

"Get out here you coward!" I yelled, pounding my hand on the door.

Luke was about to start wailing just as a shadow appeared in the corner of my eye, and I snapped my head towards the disturbance to see Mary, standing with a tray of pastries and a thunderous expression on her face.

"What the fuck are you playing at?" She stormed over and grabbed my forearm before I could land another blow on the door. "We have a plan."

I turned on her, ripping my arm free. "He hurt Luke—"

Pulling her hand away, I faced the door again, ready to tear it down myself when the handle turned and the door swung open to reveal my father, his mouth twisted downwards in a show of disapproval.

"Can I help you son?" he asked icily, his cold gaze a silent order to leave.

I turned to the side, holding out Luke's wrist for him to

see. "Your *son* has come after mine, your own flesh and blood. Or does that mean nothing to you?"

For the first time in a long time, my father was lost for words.

His jaw twitched, and he glanced inside. I could see Damien through the gap in the doorway.

"Did you do this?" my father demanded without a care for the status of those listening.

Damien rolled his eyes dismissively. "Why would I bother? Luke is harmless. This is a ridiculous, baseless accusation."

"Liar." I snarled, struggling against Mary's grip.

If it wasn't for Luke's worried expression and the tremble of his lower lip at all of the drama, I would have ripped Damien limb from limb right in front of his dead friends so he could join them.

My father studied Damien for a moment before shutting the door on me. I heard muffled voices, and my father's raised voice. At first, I thought he was done. Then, my father opened the door again and stepped outside to join us with a worn expression and gestured towards the surgery.

"We need to get that off him, now."

My father strode back towards the stairs, motioning for me to follow. Trusting my father was not something I was comfortable with, but I needed this bracelet off Luke as soon as possible. With no other choice, I hurried after him with Luke in my arms. I let my father examine Luke's arm as best he could with the child wriggling in my arms, taking care not to touch the silver. When he looked up, his eyes were shining with an emotion I'd rarely seen him display. Concern.

"I've seen something like this before. Witches have used silver as shackles over the years. At one point, they placed bracelets on werewolves before their first change in the hopes it would stop the transition. They don't work, but they cause a great deal of pain," he explained, turning Luke's wrist to examine the silver band further.

I frowned, my stomach twisting at the thought of a fellow pack member doing something so cruel. "How do we break the spell?"

"Well, we can't touch it because it sets the silver off and hurts Luke," His lips thinned and he tapped his foot, staring at the wall deep in thought until an answer came to him. "The only way to get it off is acid enchanted to break bindings."

I blanched, snatching Luke away from him. "Not a chance."

"Sorry, not the acid you're thinking of. A special mix of vampire venom with a little something will work to melt it away," he explained, patting my shoulder. "Luke won't feel a thing."

"He better not," I muttered, shrugging off his touch as I stared down at my innocent little boy and wondered how exactly we ended up in this mess.

My father disappeared out the door, most likely into the basement where he stored most of his concoctions.

I tried to hold Luke by his waist, but he was growing impatient and cranky in the run up to his bedtime. He kept rolling onto his belly, beginning to wail, kicking out and twisting in my arms until my skin ended up hitting off the bracelet.

I cursed under my breath and watched in horror as the silver burned his skin, leaving an angry red mark circling his wrist. Tears pricked the corner of my eyes as I tried to calm Luke down, cradling him against my chest and pulling my hoodie sleeves down over my hands to avoid hitting the bracelet again.

"It's ok little man, we're going to get this off you," I promised, kissing the top of his head and humming one of the lullabies Laura used to sing to him.

I was just short of yelling for my father when he reappeared with a small vial of silver liquid that glinted in the light.

"What took you so long?" I asked, dabbing Luke's wet cheeks with my sleeve. "We need this bracelet off now."

My father kneeled beside us and gently pried Luke's hand from one of the strings on my hoodie. "This won't take long."

Luke eyed him with suspicion, quickly learning that the bracelet meant pain.

"Hey mister, I need you to be a big boy for me. You can do that for grandad, can't you?" my father cooed, looking more paternal than ever.

I didn't trust him, but it worked. Luke let his grandad straighten his arm, burying his head in my chest.

"A few drops should do the job." He removed the bottle stopper and holding the dropper over the bracelet.

Holding Luke close, I watched as three drops of the silver liquid dropped onto the bracelet. A pop followed a hissing sound as the venom ate away the metal, causing it to blacken and fall away. Within seconds, the bracelet fell off Luke's wrist and hit the desk with a clang.

"All done," my father said in a sing-song voice.

I was waiting for the lollipop, but it never came.

Luke looked up at me and then at his arm, rubbing the sore red mark and wincing.

"I've something for that." My father produced a small tube of cream and rubbing it over the burn, earning a kick from Luke in the process. "With his healing, it will be gone in a matter of days."

I nodded, cradling Luke in my arms as he flopped back against me. With all the drama and crying, the kid had worn himself out. I scooped him up and walked towards the door, pausing in the doorway to look back at my father.

"Thanks."

Yes, he had helped my son, but it was under his watch the bracelet had manifested—not to mention his involvement in the death of our alpha. I felt like a traitor accepting his help or thanking him.

My father shook his head. "Don't thank me. Please, think about what you're doing."

"You think this is my fault?" I snapped, my hackles rising.

"No," he said firmly, closing up the bottle of vampire venom and picking the silver bracelet up with a cloth. "You're playing a dangerous game."

My sharp tongue got the better of me, the words tumbling out of my mouth of their own accord. "You're the one knee deep in this, not me. You did this. He's out of control and you made him that way."

The briefest hint of regret surfaced before my father's usual stoic expression returned. "I'm telling you this because I care. Back down. There's no need for you to get involved."

"Maybe you're used to having no one stand up to you. Maybe you told Damien he could be anything he wanted one time too many." I growled, shifting Luke in my arms to close the door behind me with one parting warning. "But you have blood on your hands. I won't let him ruin this pack; I owe my son a future."

CHAPTER 23

I woke with a start to the noise of someone rattling the door handle. Curled up in bed with Luke, I instinctively wrapped my arms around him to make sure he was safe. I'd spent the night moving our things into Darren's place. The pack had outgrown the manor a few years back, so during our alpha's reign, he built houses on the land behind it for each family that wanted to move out. It wasn't far, but it would have to do for now.

Luke stirred slightly, nuzzling into my chest, but he didn't wake. A familiar voice hissed my name from outside. It was then I noticed Mary's scent and noted the desperation in her voice.

Doing my best to keep him asleep, I scooped Luke into my arms and gently transferred him to the cot, wrapping a baby blanket around him and tucking his wolf teddy in beside him. I held my breath when he mumbled something in gibberish, but he soon fell silent, the gentle rise and fall of his chest resuming.

"Tom, please," Mary, who was able to hear every single

movement of mine from outside the door, whispered again. Panic laced her every word. "I know you're awake. I need your help."

I threw on a dirty T-shirt as I snuck across the room and pulled the door open to see Mary standing in the corridor, tears streaming down her face. Her shoulders slumped and smudged mascara circled her wild eyes.

"Please, you need to come now," she pleaded, grabbing my forearm with a vice like grip. "Cormac's locked himself in his room, and he won't open the door."

I looked over my shoulder at Luke sleeping peacefully in his cot. "Are you sure he hasn't just fallen asleep?"

"No." Her lower lip began to tremble, and she wrapped her arms around her torso. "Something is wrong, I can feel it."

"Okay, okay. I'm coming."

Cursing under my breath, I snuck back into the room to grab a pair of runners, pausing briefly beside the cot to place a light kiss on Luke's cheek. A heavy weight settled on my shoulders as I clicked the door shut behind me. I waited but no crying came. Mary was waiting impatiently in the hallway, like a horse ready to bolt.

"Darren?" I said, rapping on his door as we rushed past. "I need you to mind Luke."

He opened his door a minute later, hair ruffled and groggy as hell. "Sure... What's going on?"

"Cormac's missing," I explained, shoving my runners on while Mary danced on the spot. "Call Aoife to watch Luke and then come find us. Keep Shane here too."

As we left Darren's house, I saw the moon on the cusp of its full cycle hanging ominously over the manor. The night air was cool, the only noise coming from the breeze ruffling the trees and the old rusting gate to the rose garden creaking back and forth.

Jogging to the house wasn't fast enough for Mary. She broke into a sprint, slamming the back door open as she raced through without missing a beat. I kept pace with her, my trainers squeaking on the floors as we raced through the manor and took the stairs two at a time.

The winding staircase leading to the top floor seemed to take forever, the angled steps forcing me to take smaller steps.

"Where were your father and Damien all night?"

It wasn't a question; it was an accusation.

"My father was called out on an emergency. I can't speak for Damien or what he got up to after his vamp friends left."

She muttered something under her breath.

"I'm telling the truth. I took the call and then a friend from the hospital texted about seeing my father." I met her level gaze. "I don't trust my father either, but I can't lie to make him fit the bill."

Mary's eyes narrowed a fraction, but she didn't argue, taking me at my word despite her cool tone. We didn't have time to argue.

"Cormac?" I called, skidding to a stop outside his room and banging my fist on the door. "Open the door."

There was no answer.

"Come on man, you're freaking out your sister." I pressed my ear to the wood and straining my hearing, but the only noise was Mary stopping beside me, her breathing laboured. My chest tightened, and I knocked on the door again, raising my voice. "Cormac! Quit playing!"

Mary wore a sickly expression, her freckles pale, and sweat beading her brow.

"Stand back," I said, taking a handful of steps backwards.

"Wha—"

Before she could finish her question, I ran full tilt at the door. My shoulder slammed into the it, knocking the door clean off the hinges and sending wood splintering as it crashed onto the floor. I rushed into the room, closely followed by Mary. It was empty.

She hurried past me to check the bathroom. Just like Mary's, the room was split in two parts, a large open plan living room with a small kitchen, more like a studio. Everything was untouched. I followed her, noticing his bed was made, and the lights were off. There was no sign of Cormac. She emerged from her search, her expression a pained mix of worry and anger, shaking her head and flopping onto his bed in defeat.

"He wouldn't pull a prank like this, not after mam and dad." Her voice was barely a broken whisper. "Where is he?"

"Could he have gone out to blow off steam?"

"Not a chance, he's been keeping close since the hunt." She shook her head, shooting daggers at me for merely suggesting such a thing. "I'm telling you, I saw him heading upstairs."

I sighed, half-heartedly rummaging through the contents on his desk but there was nothing out of place. "He's not here, it doesn't even look like he came back. Why wouldn't he just go to bed?"

"If I knew that, I wouldn't have come for help," she snapped, throwing her hands up in frustration. "How do you explain his door being locked?"

She has a point.

Mary rolled her eyes at my perplexed response. "Exactly."

She rose to her feet, the mattress bouncing as she stood, followed by a quiet thud. Frowning, she crouched by the bed and reached underneath for whatever had fallen. When she raised her head, her complexion was white and her eyes round with sheer terror.

"What is it?" I asked, skirting around the bed to join her.

She clutched a small pill bottle in her hand, except it wasn't paracetamol. The moment she popped the lid I could smell it. *Nightshade.*

The bottle was empty, only a pinch of the ground up herb remaining.

"We have to find him, *now.*"

CHAPTER 24

Once we had alerted the pack, which involved a lot of yelling and hammering on every door in the main house, we let them wake the rest of the estate while we searched the manor. My father was readying an antidote under Darren's watchful gaze, Aoife was minding Luke. We were trying to keep the children out of this mess. Mary and I had deliberated for all of a minute, conscious of my father's involvement and the fact there was a traitor in the pack, but we had no choice. That amount of nightshade was lethal. We needed to find Cormac.

There was no sign of him anywhere; the library was empty, and the kitchens were untouched. An eerie sense of dread had nestled in my gut, and every time we checked a new spot and Cormac wasn't there, the knot of tension expanded. Time was ticking, and we had no idea where he was.

Leaving Mary to keep scouting through the spare rooms, I jogged back upstairs. I passed my father, giving him a brief run down before continuing on the third floor and checking Cormac's room once more. Whether my father was involved or not, we needed an antidote, and we needed it yesterday.

Cormac's scent was all over the place, which didn't help. I couldn't track a fresh trail from his room even though I was probably one of the best trackers the pack had, I was coming up blank.

I rubbed my eyes with the back of my hand, bracing one hand against the wall and stared out the window. His room had one of the best views of the rolling estate and the meadow stretching to the forest tree line. Under the light of the full moon, I could see people darting from one house to the other to wake the rest of the pack. Their distant shouts and desperate yells echoed to where I was.

My phone buzzed in my back pocket, but as I reached for it, my shaking hands fumbled with the device and it fell, bouncing off the windowsill and landing on the floor. I crouched down to pick it up, Damien's name flashing on the screen, and that's when I noticed it—another fresh scent trail on the window and the handle.

I scrambled to get the window open and leaned out. Their cent was on the outside ledge and then vanished. The drop must have been about twenty feet onto a grassy verge. Possibly fatal to a human, a breeze for a werewolf—but for one with nightshade in their system?

We had to move fast. From what I remembered of my father's teachings, we had maybe a half an hour.

"Mary!" I yelled, not breaking pace as I bolted out of the room, taking the stairs at full speed until I practically crashed into her on the first floor. I grabbed her by the shoulders, my words strung together. "Cormac jumped out his window, that's why I couldn't figure out where he went. We need to search outside."

I made a beeline for the quickest exit, racing through the dining room and into the function room. Mary was hot on my heels as I forced open the patio doors, the early summer breeze washing over me as we stepped out under the stars. We took a sharp right, running around the outside of the house, stopping directly under Cormac's bedroom window. I inhaled deeply, immediately picking up signs of Cormac. A werewolf's sense of smell isn't an exact science, I couldn't tell how long ago he left, but it had been nearly twenty minutes since Mary knocked on my door, and I couldn't get a straight answer on how long she had been trying to find him. It sent her into a spiral of panic. We were running out of time.

Inhaling deeply, I focused on Cormac's scent, and I was about to shift when movement to my right caught my eye.

"Father told me about Cormac. Do you need help?" Damien asked, his irritating rat-like face coming into view as he rounded the corner of the back porch.

"Why don't you tell us where he is and stop wasting our time?" I snapped, shoving past him and motioning for Mary to follow.

"How dare you speak to me like that." He stiffened, his fists clenching and unclenching by his side.

Before I could get another word in, Mary strode right up to Damien with a face like thunder. She was at least a foot smaller, but she squared up to him without a hint of fear.

"My brother is in danger, and I know you're responsible," she spat, her words laced with venom. She prodded him firmly in the chest with an extended claw for good measure. "If we don't get to him in time, I'll kill you myself."

Damien's lips twisted into the most sadistic of smiles, amusement sparking in his coal eyes. "Careful now. Making threats like that is what gets people into trouble."

Mary let out a guttural scream, but before she could launch herself at him, I cut in and grabbed her by the wrist. "As much as I'd love to see you tear his head off, it won't help us find Cormac. He's not going to tell us anything."

It didn't surprise me one bit how blasé he was being about the whole thing. With Cormac out of the picture, Damien would have the whole thing sown up nice and neat. His callousness and the sheer lack of empathy was still jarring. To think I'd grown up with him in a sense turned my stomach.

"Tom is right, run along now," Damien purred, making a shooing motion. "The clock is ticking."

Mary tensed and her eyes flashed silver. I could sense her magic beginning to surge.

"Fuck off." I growled, finding the only words fitting for a psychopath like him.

Damien's laugh was cruel, and it took every ounce of control I had to drag a shaking Mary away from him and focus on finding her brother.

Casting out my senses, I zoned in on Cormac's scent and started pulling his sister in the direction of the trail. It was fresh and gradually growing stronger. The damp grass soaked my trainers as we ran through the gardens, the ground soft and loamy as we reached the edge of the forest. The full moon hung high above us, shards of light filtering through the canopy as if it were lighting our way.

Mary followed in silence, responding to my cues, her haunted gaze mirroring my own fears. I thought about shifting, but one look at her told me she would follow suit, and she wasn't in control. Besides, Cormac's scent only became clearer as we picked our way through the undergrowth.

We were close.

I heard the creek babbling to my right and dread settled in my gut as I realised what direction we were headed in. The path Cormac had taken was all too familiar. I might have the best nose, but Cormac's scent had grown strong enough for Mary to know he was close. The canopy thinned as we neared a clearing, and I reached an arm out behind me, catching her mid-step.

"Wait here," I whispered, uncertainty threading through my voice.

She nodded slowly, her wide eyes fixed on the darkness ahead. Silent tears began rolling down her cheeks as if she already knew.

I swallowed hard and started walking towards the clearing. With each step I took, my legs felt heavy, as if the undergrowth was pulling me back. Images flashed through my mind, visions of my alpha and the pyre alight in the centre of the clearing. I could almost smell burning wood in the air, but instead, it was so much worse.

On the far side of the clearing, a large branch creaked under the weight of Cormac's lifeless body swaying in the wind. My stomach lurched, and I raced over to the base of the tree, supporting his body with one arm while I slashed the noose with the extended claws of my free hand. His head hung limp in my arms, his skin blotchy and purple where the rope had sliced into his neck. I lowered him to the ground and frantically checked for a pulse, but I was too late. He was dead.

I staggered backwards, a loud roar of anguish ripping from my throat. Wood splintered around my fist as it slammed into the tree.

A shrill scream came from behind me. I turned to see Mary rushing forwards, her face contorted in agony as she wailed and sprinted towards her brother's motionless body. I grabbed her by the waist as she ran past and pulled her back, keeping a firm grip despite her thrashing until she collapsed sobbing in my arms, her ghostly cries echoing through the forest.

CHAPTER 25

Driving into the city this late at night was eerie. The winding country roads, dark and empty, gave way to streets busy with taxis and the distant base beats of the clubs bursting with late night revellers. Bright streetlamps and headlights obscured the blanket of stars hanging high in the sky, and only the moon was distinguishable, its light casting shadows on the river Liffey splitting the city in two. Coasting on autopilot, I drove through the winding streets until I pulled up outside a familiar set of apartments, and the engine stuttered to a halt.

I took a long, deep breath and exhaled slowly, bracing my hands on the steering wheel. My heart was still thumping out of my chest, and my palms were slick. I couldn't stop my hands shaking. Despite the noise and sirens, Luke didn't stir.

"Breathe," I muttered to myself, climbing out of the car and easing Luke's door open quietly in the hopes of keeping him asleep.

Of course, I wasn't quiet enough. Ambulance sirens might not have woken him, but one movement from me and Luke's eyes fluttered open. He clutched his wolf teddy to his face and squinted as the glare of a streetlight stung his eyes. Before I could get him out of the car seat, he gave a signature sniffle before bursting into tears.

I cradled Luke against my chest, nuzzling the top of his head as I slung the rucksack full of essentials I'd grabbed over my shoulder. My phone buzzed in my pocket, and I flicked it out to see a text from Shane saying that he and Darren weren't far behind me.

It was probably for the best I'd left first. If I'd stayed a moment longer, I'd have strangled Damien in front of my son. Darren would eventually coax Mary into leaving, and everything would be fine. I just needed to remember to breathe.

"We'll be alright," I murmured softly, nudging the car door closed with my hip, carrying Luke to the apartment building.

I'd turned up to Helena before, but never like this. Never with a child in tow. We had nowhere else to go. I had been in such a rush to get out of the manor, I didn't bother ringing ahead, but when I dialled Helena's buzzer, she answered immediately.

"Tom, come straight up," her familiar voice rang through.

Shane must have contacted Gráinne; of course she'd give her friend a heads up.

I wasn't sure how much Helena knew, but she was hovering at the door to her apartment by the time I stepped out of the lift. She let me scoot past and watched as I set a groggy Luke down on the couch. When I turned to her with my arms free, she flung hers around my neck.

"I'm so glad you're okay." Her voice was hoarse with worry. "Gráinne told me about Cormac."

I sighed and nuzzled into her neck, inhaling her calming

scent. "I'm sorry. I didn't have any time to let you know what was happening. Things changed so fast..."

"Don't be sorry, you did what you had to do."

With that, she untangled herself from our embrace, and I turned to Luke who was now slouching and staring at the two of us with an expression that was a cross between amusement and confusion. Not that he had any idea what was going on, but it still made me chuckle ever so slightly.

"Wolf?" Luke asked, holding out his teddy to Helena.

She shook her head, giving the teddy an enthusiastic pat on the head. "He's lovely. I'm not a wolf, but I hear you're going to be a big strong werewolf when you grow up."

He beamed up at her and thrust his teddy into her hand, his signature sign of approval. I bit back a smile at the exchange, the sight of his innocence warming my heart.

Helena sat down on the couch beside Luke, adjusting the blanket I'd wrapped around his shoulders. "Right little man, this is going to have to do as your bed tonight."

"Sorry about landing all of this on you," I said, perching on the arm of the couch.

She raised a hand to stop me. "Apologise once more, and I'll kick you out."

Luke stuck his tongue out when he recognised I was being chastised.

I blew a heavy breath and shook my head. "Yes ma'am."

All jokes aside, the situation really was a mess. We tucked Luke in on the couch and left him curled up, kept safe by a mound of pillows blocking the edge while we went into the kitchen to make the hot chocolate Helena had promised him. I watched her go about the kitchen, my mind racing through the events of the last 48 hours, trying to figure out how I'd gotten things so wrong. I should have stopped Damien before it came to this.

"It's not your fault." Helena's voice pierced my spiralling thoughts.

I sighed and braced my hands on the kitchen counter. "Then why does it feel like it is?"

"Because you are a good person. Too good maybe." She walked over to set down the carton of milk in her hand and wound her arms around my waist, nestling her chin in the hollow between my shoulder blades. "You're shouldering everyone else's problems, on top of your own."

I shrugged, spinning in place to rest my hands on her hips. "I feel like my problems pale in comparison. Mary has lost her whole family."

"And you lost your wife," she said softly, brushing a stray hair behind my ear.

I swallowed hard. "I will always love Laura, but I can't play the widower card forever."

"You're not playing a card Tom. You've been hurt too." Helena shook her head, giving me a disapproving look. "You came home to mend your relationship with your father only to find out your alpha was murdered due to scheme your father and half-brother are involved in. You're losing your family too."

Her words hit home harder than I expected.

I stared at those piercing emerald eyes full of empathy.

"I get it." She cupped my cheek. "Leaving my family was the hardest thing I ever had to do."

"Why did you leave?"

She paused for a moment, chewing over her answer. "Some people aren't meant to have kids. My dad was a gambler and an alcoholic, he wasn't a good person. He hit my mother, and she was so hooked on alcohol she didn't care. They were a mess."

"I'm sorry." I wrapped my arms around her waist to pull

her closer, inhaling deeply as her calming scent filled my senses. "You deserved better."

"Sometimes you have to make your family. Gráinne is like a sister, I've got good friends, and now I have you too." Her voice lost its edge as she spoke more fondly of her friends.

I couldn't stop the smile, which was at odds with the overall situation, curving my lips. This moment felt like a cosy bubble I wanted to stay in forever.

"I know it's only been a few months, but," I began, fumbling for the right words, my palms growing slick when I realised what I was about to say. "I love you."

Her eyes widened, and she placed her delicate hand over mine. "I love you, too."

She leaned up to press her lips to mine. It wasn't a hungry kiss but tender and full of meaning. My heart thumped in my chest as I lost myself in the moment, tangling my hand in her hair and pulling her close.

When Helena pulled away, her cheeks were flushed pink.

"I never thought I'd feel this way again." I nudged her nose with mine, my lips curving at the way her blush only deepened.

She smiled, returning the gesture. "I never thought I'd feel like this either. I always thought that soulmate stuff was a load of crap, and it probably is."

I arched a comical brow, and she laughed.

"I'm not saying I want to run off into the sunset with you and we'll live some fairy-tale life," she joked, her tone turning thoughtful. "But I want to try this."

"Even if my pack is a mess and my world is nothing like yours?"

She rolled her eyes, prodding me gently in the chest. "You might be a werewolf, but there's a human element to everyone. You're not some immortal god, even if you all drive like one."

"I always wondered how humans came to terms with our

world," I mused aloud, studying her carefully. "Some lose their minds, some pretend it was all in their imagination, but a select few dive straight in. Maybe they're stubborn, crazy even."

"Or in love," she added, amusement sparkling in her eyes. "And not scared off by ghost stories."

"Ghosts are the least of our worries."

We both laughed morbidly, and I leaned in for another kiss, but the noise of the apartment buzzer, followed by Luke wailing at the disturbance to his sleep, killed what was left of our moment.

"I'll get the door," Helena said with a disappointed sigh, giving me a peck on the cheek before unwinding herself from my embrace. "You sort the hot chocolate and something stronger for the adults."

Moments later, Darren strode into the kitchen with Luke balanced on his hip, closely followed by Mary, who was clutching her brother's hoodie and visibly shaking.

I guided her to a chair and shared a worried look with Helena, who was already making something to calm Mary down.

"Sorry we took so long." He plopped into a chair with a heavy sigh, the wooden legs scrapping against the kitchen tiles. "I had one last thing to take care of."

I frowned, grabbing the hot chocolate out of the microwave after it pinged. "What did you do?"

The others filed into the room, Shane holding a pale Gráinne's hand and Helena leading the rear. Shane's shoulders hunched, and I could tell by the way his mouth was set in a thin line that he wasn't impressed with his brother.

"I just left Damien a message, something to keep him occupied," Darren said with a nonchalant shrug.

Luke held out his hands, doing a grabby motion as I walked over to him with the mug of lukewarm hot chocolate.

"What did you do?" I asked, not so sure I wanted to know the answer.

Darren didn't answer, simply sitting there like a bold child. Eventually, Shane ratted him out.

"He decked Damien and called the cops, so now the humans and the witches are there keeping him busy."

I shook my head and sighed.

For once, Darren's temper may have bought us some time.

I never imagined I'd end up in this situation, trying to save my pack, but after what had happened with Damien, I wasn't sure how well I knew anything anymore. Despite everything, there was an unshakeable feeling in my gut telling me coming home had been the right thing. It made me cringe, because I was no hero, I was a mess.

Looking around the table felt surreal. We all huddled in Helena's kitchen after I put Luke to bed on the couch, each one of us looking as shaken as the next. Three werewolves, two humans, and a hybrid baby ready to drop at any moment. Mary stayed silent as I explained what happened to Cormac. Shane sat next to Gráinne with a grim expression, one arm wrapped around her shoulder while she cradled her baby bump protectively. Darren was so angry he kept switching between sitting and staring at the table with a burning intensity, and then jumping up and pacing around the room, getting in Helena's way as she moved about making tea for everyone. She was the only one functioning at this point.

The apartment buzzer rang and all of us bar Helena jumped.

"Brilliant, pizza's here," she announced, drawing me out of my nightmarish daydreams.

Shane's tummy grumbled, but he looked sickly and shook his head. "I don't think I could stomach anything."

Darren just shrugged. Nothing would ever put him off food, and I had to admit I was feeling a bit lightheaded. What with everything going on, I'd skipped eating all day. I was so busy trying to look after everyone that my own needs hadn't even registered. Mary looked like she was about to puke, but she needed to eat something.

"You all need to eat," Helena insisted, placing her hands on her hips. "We need you thinking straight before we can make a plan."

"We don't have a plan." Darren sighed, his usual snarky remarks absent.

"I know, but if you guys want to fix this mess, you need one."

With that, Helena walked out of the room, and I could hear a click as she pressed the button releasing the door downstairs. A minute later, the smell of cheese and doughy goodness filtered into the room. Helena thanked the delivery girl quietly, keeping her voice low to avoid waking Luke before easing the door closed.

Only then did my senses kick in, and I leaped out of my seat, rushing to help her carry the pizzas. Chivalry had obviously died along with my pack as she was already in the kitchen doorway by the time I swung into motion.

"Relax." She chuckled softly, placing a reassuring hand on my arm as my expression crumpled. "I can manage these. You grab some plates."

With a renewed sense of purpose, I rummaged around in the cupboards and produced a stack of plates. Doing something so simple felt like a ridiculous achievement when my world had come to a standstill.

I watched in awe as Helena moved around unpacking the pizzas and grabbing cutlery. The room had fallen silent in her absence. She was the only thing breathing life and hope into our unusual group of bandits.

Once the pizza was in front of us, our stomachs roared into life and Darren finished off one pizza by himself. Mary picked at a slice and eventually found her appetite, though it did little to bring colour back to her cheeks. Even Gráinne managed a small smile at the sight of Shane's face covered in sauce, just like his brother.

Once we were sat around with full stomachs, I could tell from the look Helena gave me that we needed to get down to business.

"I know a lot has happened..." I began, struggling to find the right words. "But we can't leave Damien in charge of the pack. He'll destroy it. We have to go back and prove that he's behind everything. If not for Cormac, then for Mary."

Darren slumped in his chair, rubbing his face with his palm. "How are we going to do that? You've been trying to find proof for ages. He's impossible to catch out."

"Even if we prove it, the pack might not listen," Shane said, his tone grim.

I shrugged, splaying my hands on the table. "We're just going to have to show our hand and hope the pack can see through him, even if some of them listen, it's better than him reigning over the largest pack in Ireland. Who knows what he's got planned?"

"Nothing good." Darren flicked an empty garlic mayonnaise tub across his pizza box.

Mary shook her head, rising shakily to her feet. She braced her hands on the table and fixed me with a gaze of fierce determination. "With the witches on his side, proving Damien is a murderer won't be enough. If the pack won't listen, you need to stop him."

"Me?" I pointed at myself in disbelief. "No, I'm not the answer to this."

"Yes, you are. My father always said you were a fantastic leader."

"I'm no leader! This is madness, I'm not going to be their alpha."

She straightened up, slowly looking around our little group. "Damien won't stop until you're dead."

The room fell silent.

"I'm not talking about murder, and I don't like the idea any more than the rest of you," Mary said, taking a shallow breath. Hurt laced her words but there was a resigned certainty there too. "Tom needs to fight under the next full moon, and he needs to win. It's the only way."

I swallowed hard.

Yes, it was the only way without any repercussions, but I wasn't a killer. I was angry, furious, but the thought of taking someone's life—even someone as evil as Damien—made the pizza in my stomach somersault. My son was in the next room, and here we were discussing *killing* a man.

"Tom, please." Tears clogger her throat as Mary reached out across the table to place a shaky hand on mine. "It's the only way to end this nightmare. The witches can't stop you fighting him. Larissa decreed it herself."

I rubbed my face with my hand, wishing I could wake up from the reality I found myself in. "I need time to think."

"We don't have time. It's barely a week away," Darren piped up, shooting me a sombre smile.

Looking around at my friends, I could see all of them were considering Mary's plan. Even Helena was mulling it over. The way she inclined her head in the slightest of nods told me she was on board with the idea.

Was I the only one who thought this was insane?

Darren took a long sip of the beer he'd helped himself to and sighed. "He's never going to stop."

"He went after Luke," Helena said, walking over to wrap a supportive arm around my waist. "This is the only way to keep your family safe."

Shane shook his head, his confusion mirroring Gráinne's. "Wait, I know Darren said Damien was responsible for the alpha's death, but I thought he paid the witches off or something...."

"No, he killed our alpha with his own hands. He staged Cormac's death to look like a suicide, but he forced the poison down his throat," I explained, my tone growing cold. "He's a murderer, and it's clear he'll stop at nothing to ensure he's the alpha."

"I never thought I'd say this, but I agree with Mary." Darren spoke up, his jaw ticking. "He's just going to keep killing until he gets his way."

Gráinne paled even further, one hand clutching Shane's hand while the other rubbed her belly. "She's not safe."

"No, you and the baby can't stay with the pack, not until all of this is sorted," I agreed, drumming my fingers on the table.

For the first time that evening, Helena's expression faltered. I reached out and pulled her close.

"All I have is the pack. My family is the pack." Panic rose in Shane's voice as he looked between his brother and the mother of his unborn child.

It was Gráinne who finally spoke up with a solution, her voice thick with emotion.

"I have family in Scotland, we can go stay with them for a while," she suggested, sounding surer with each word. "They're really nice and mam was already angry about the baby. She even suggested we run off to Gretna Green."

"The old ferry-boat-and-return-with-a-ring plan," Helena muttered, her shoulders slumping.

Gráinne gave her friend a reproachful look. "It's not forever, and it's not that far either. You could visit anytime."

"You can't fly." Darren looked rather surprised at his own knowledge of pregnant women. "It's too late in your pregnancy, you've got less than six weeks left."

They all looked to me and then back to Darren in surprise when I shrugged. "You'd get away with it, but there's a chance the flight could trigger labour."

"There's a ferry to England, and you can drive up to Scotland," Helena said, clearly reluctant to give them an out. "It's a long car ride, but you can just rent a car over there and maybe stay overnight along the way."

The look of dread slowly left Shane's face as he smiled and looked around the group, giving Gráinne's hand a reassuring squeeze. "Sounds like we have a plan."

"Do we?" Mary asked, her question loaded.

I looked around the table and exhaled slowly, trying to ignore the unshakeable sense of dread swirling in the pit of my stomach when I realised I had no other choice. If it came to it, killing Damien was our only way out.

"We have a plan."

CHAPTER 27

Skulking around alleyways at this hour of night never felt good. The light sheet of rain coupled with the grimy cobbles and graffitied walls only cemented the feeling. It was the only time Niamh would agree to meet, and we were racing against the clock as the full moon would peak in a few days. A cool breeze circled, biting into my skin, but I kept my head down and my eyes trained on Darren's hulking figure ahead of me. With his hoodie up and his broad shoulders, he looked like trouble.

The roofs of buildings lining the alley jutted out just enough to offer some shelter from the weather. We passed two men lurking in the shadows cutting some sort of deal, but their hushed whispering was no match for my ears. Not your usual drug deal though, if the vile of blood passed from one hand to another was anything to go by.

Darren disappeared around the corner. When he came back into view, he was standing beside a familiar bricked wall and an old, rusted door that looked like it was ready to crumble at the slightest touch. He wasted no time in banging his fist on the door, subtle as ever.

I pulled my hoodie sleeves down further, quickly checking my phone for messages from Helena while the door warped and worked its magic. Leaving Luke with her had felt weird, but I trusted her, and Luke seemed to love all of the attention. This was no place for a kid, and I'd already dragged him into too much drama. He needed to stay safe.

"We don't have all day. If we leave it too long, she'll bolt," Darren warned.

I sighed and stuffed my phone in my back pocket as I hurried after him, entering through the new doorway. Inside, the corridor was guarded by two tall men standing either side.

Before we reached them, something launched itself off the wall with a shriek and landed in front of us. Darren jumped back, bumping into me in the process, a low growl ripping from his throat.

"What the fuck?" Darren snapped, his eyes flashing silver.

In front of us was a mid-sized gargoyle slowly shedding its stone exterior to expose its wrinkled hairless skin, much like that of a bat's wing.

One of the men standing guard—Baz—sprang into action, quickly manifesting in front of the ugly creature. "Stop Orfeo. Stand down."

"Marked." The gargoyle hissed, a forked tongue striking out. Its rounded black eyes stared up at us.

"No, not marked. I've known Tom for years," Baz said, his own body rippling slightly as his glamour slipped to reveal his demonic form in a show of warning. "Stand down."

The gargoyle shot us another chilling look before beginning to retreat down the hall, its clawed feet clicking as it moved and disappeared somewhere to the left.

"What was that?" I asked, turning to the demon who had intervened.

"A new alarm system they've been testing out." Baz

chuckled as he caught the incredulous look on Darren's face. "It's faulty in my opinion."

I shook my head, brushing my hair back as I exhaled heavily. "I prefer the old system. Thanks for stepping in."

If it wasn't for the stench of demon in the air, you'd never know Baz was a demon with those sparkling blue eyes. In the paranormal world, thanks to magic and glamours, nothing was ever as it seemed.

The demon nodded sharply and gestured towards the door marking the end of the corridor. "Anytime. I saw a friend of yours sneak in a few minutes ago. No trouble please."

Darren and I shared a look before thanking him once more and heading in the direction we were prompted. The noise levels exploded as I pushed the door open to see the venue in full swing. Supernatural creatures of every kind dotted around tables, strutting their stuff on the dance floor, and queuing for drinks. There was a mixture, some glamoured, some not. We were here for business though, so I immediately focused and picked apart the different scents to zero in on a small snug in the far corner.

I motioned for Darren to follow and strode up to the snug, placing my hands on the shoulders of a young woman with fiery red curls tumbling down her back. "Hello, Niamh."

She didn't so much as flinch, her only reaction a surge in the energy around us and a small shock of electricity shooting through the palms of my hand.

It was me who flinched.

"Good to see you again, Tom," she said, spinning in her seat to greet us with a wide smile.

Niamh was a powerful witch, but she kept her powers tightly under wraps and masked them well. It was only on the few occasions I'd seen her lose her temper that I got even the smallest glimpse into what she was capable of. Her history was a mystery, but there were rumours.

Darren peeked out from behind me with an awkward wave. "Did you miss me?"

"So, he brought you along, too." Her smile dropped and she pursed her lips, those striking blue cat eyes of hers slowly looking Darren up and down before turning to me once more. "Did you think I'd go soft and drop the price?"

I shook my head, shooting Darren a warning look. He'd pestered me to come, and I knew it wasn't a good idea. I should've gone with my gut. She must have been twice our age at least, but she didn't look it at all. I'd warned him off her so many times, but the man was happy to play with fire.

"No, I'd never ask you to do that." I slid onto the small couch-chair on the opposite side of the table and meeting her level gaze. "I'm not an idiot."

She hooked her thumb over her shoulder. "He is."

Darren's cool-as-a-cucumber act slipped ever so slightly before he rolled his shoulders and slapped on his lopsided grin, sliding in beside me. "Niamh, if we could just... I know I screw—"

Niamh held up a delicate but deadly hand to stop his babbling. "You screwed that Fae. She didn't put some spell on you. Man up, it was just a bit of fun."

He nodded and promptly shut his mouth.

Once she was done enjoying his discomfort, Niamh reached into her bag and subtly slid thick, brown envelope across the table to me. "It's time to get down to business."

I caught the envelope, opening it to take a quick peek and received a stinging slap to the hand, so I stuffed it into my hoodie pocket.

"You'd be a shit dealer."

"Good thing I'm not into the black market," I muttered, rubbing the back of my hand.

Niamh never just slapped—there was always a nasty sting of magic.

She rolled her eyes, shifting forwards in her seat to lean across the table. "I felt bad about not getting you the information on Damien in time, so I managed to do a bit more digging. I went to pay that Garda another visit."

"Garda Brennan?" I said, shifting closer.

"Yeah, Mary's vamp friend wasn't old enough to notice there was a spell blocking his memories. It had Larissa's touch all over it," Niamh explained, wrinkling her nose in disgust. "He did see Fiachra that night, but Damien was there too, with blood on his hands."

Darren sighed in frustration. "It's their word against ours though."

She shook her head and pushed a second envelope across the table with a mischievous smirk. "I have him on record. There's a voice recording and a signed statement. I thought about bringing the man himself, but kidnapping a human wasn't covered in the fee."

I peeked at the contents and, true to her word, there was a voice recorder and statements implicating Damien. I wondered what the royals would make of this if I brought up what Larissa was doing. They were cruel, but they valued rules. Larissa had a tendency to bend them.

"Now, back to the main reason you're here." Niamh reverted to her more business-like tone. "There's two passports in there, everything they need for a new life and identity. When the baby is born, give me a call, and I'll sort one for her, but they'd be better off legally registering her over there. I even threw in new degree certificates for Shane, so he can pick up a job, along with a lease for a flat in Edinburgh. I know you have links with the Scottish pack, but it's there just in case. The car rental is already sorted and there's contact details for a friend of mine over there if they do find themselves in trouble."

"Why would they be in trouble? You said you'd make this untraceable," Darren asked, his bushy eyebrows furrowing.

Niamh stiffened. "I said I'd do my part and get them a new life that *should* be untraceable, but I can't account for all the variables and, from what I've heard, you're dealing with one sneaky son of a bitch."

"I just want my brother to be safe," Darren mumbled, heaving a sigh.

Niamh's expression softened and for just a moment, they shared an intimate look of understanding as she reached out and gently touched his hand. "I've done my best; the rest is out of our hands."

CHAPTER 28

The wind whipped around us, and a chill set in my bones as I watched the sun peak above the ocean line, colouring the sky a pinkish red at odds with the grey of the gathering clouds. The large ferry in front of us obscured the rest of the view, an ugly eyesore docked in the pier. I could taste the salt in the air and the fresh breeze ensured I was wide awake despite getting no sleep. I'd spent the whole night tossing and turning, worrying.

We were a sombre sight gathered together that morning. Mary had returned to the pack despite me arguing the danger several times. She had refused to stay and insisted it was her responsibility to ensure her brother got a proper send off. Helena was in deep conversation with Gráinne, holding her by the shoulders so that it almost looked like some kind of pep talk. From what I could catch over the roar of the wind, it was. Judging by the set of Helena's jaw, I could tell she was biting back tears, whereas Gráinne hadn't stopped crying all morning. Darren and Shane stood close by, chatting quietly but not saying much because neither had the right words.

Spring was slow to take hold—while the sky was clear, the breeze on the pier was cutting. Only a handful of cars were waiting to board the ferry. We were second in line and while everyone else sat in their cars where they were warm, we'd all been restless within minutes and decided to brave the cold. You couldn't say goodbye stuffed in separate cars anyway and if Darren didn't get to pace around, he might have put a hole in the car window.

A small hand patted my leg.

"Daddy?" Luke asked, his big brown eyes staring up at me.

I leaned down, coming to his level and straightening his jacket that we'd had to buy that morning when the wind changed. In my haste to leave the manor, I'd packed whatever I could grab. His mother would have known what to take. She was thorough, I was the hot head.

Luke swatted at my hands, displeased with my fussing, and pointed towards the ferry. "Boad?"

"Boat," I said softly, a smile kicking up the corners of my lips. "We used to see small ones on the river in London, remember?"

He cocked his head as if deep in thought before something new and shiny caught his eye. A seagull.

Before his little legs could spur into motion, I grabbed Luke by the shoulders and scooped him up into my arms. When I looked up, I was surprised to see Gráinne walking towards me.

"How are you feeling?" I asked, immediately cringing at my stupid choice of words.

She felt like shit, we all did.

"Not great," she mumbled, shrugging with a resigned sigh. "I need to ask you something."

"You can ask me anything."

She chewed her lip, bringing one hand to rest on her

blooming baby bump, the other supporting her back. The bump almost engulfed her petite frame. "This baby is going to be a hybrid, I'm a human... How am I going to guide her through all of this?"

I rubbed my chin, trying to find the right answer as both a doctor and a friend. "You're her mother. I know we describe the pack as our family, but we are a meshwork of tight-knit families. Your baby will love and respect you as her mam, whether you can shift or not. Shane will teach her to shift, and most hybrids don't shift until their teens, so she will be old enough to understand."

"But... I can never share that with her." Gráinne looked down, gently stroking her stomach. "What if she needs me, and I can't help because I'm human?"

"Shane will teach her control, but that doesn't mean she won't learn a tonne of useful lessons from her mother. Strength and compassion among other things. There's more to being a wolf than just being able to shift." I gestured to Luke, who was content in my arms while watching the bird swoop past. "You won't be raising her alone, that's something I had to learn. We are your family too now, you can always call on us."

Gráinne was on the verge of tears again as she stepped forwards and pulled me into an awkward hug. "Thank you, for everything."

A loud siren sounded, muting my reply. Gráinne recoiled and winced as she covered her ears, while Luke erupted into tears at the harsh noise that startled the seagulls he was watching.

"It's ok," I murmured, rubbing Luke's back and rummaging around in my pocket for his toy car to distract him.

Darren walked over, his expression grim. "It's time."

The other's joined us by Shane's new car, a middle-aged Ford estate that would get them from A to B. We had decided renting a car there was too risky, it was imperative Damien didn't find out about them. Even in the future, we wanted them untraceable until we fixed the problems in the Faolchúnna pack and got rid of Damien and his disgusting ideas.

"Me and Tom sorted these for you." Darren produced the envelope filled with their passports and boarding passes, along with everything else Niamh had supplied. "You've still kept your own first names, but you're now the O'Connor's."

Shane chuckled, though it sounded off. "A good Irish name, smart choice bro."

"It's not like you can hide your accents." Darren teased, but the light didn't reach his eyes.

They shared a look that made my stomach tie itself in knots.

Gráinne took the envelope and threw her arms around Darren to all of our surprise. By the way his eyebrows shot up, he was shocked too.

"Thank you for helping us Darren." Fresh tears rolled down her cheeks as she embraced him. "I promise you will get to see your niece as soon as it's safe."

Darren throat bobbed at the use of the word niece, a fresh dose of the gravity of the situation hitting him all over again.

Shane walked over to me and gave me a hefty pat on the back as we hugged. "Thanks for everything Tom. We'll check in with that doctor once we're settled."

I'd given him the number of a werewolf I'd met while on a rotation up north. He was a trustworthy guy who would make sure Gráinne was looked after with no questions. The Hippocratic oath held firm for wolves too.

Luke reached out for a hug too, and Shane obliged with a smile.

"Good, he's trustworthy. Mention my name and he'll sort you out," I said, juggling Luke from one arm to the other.

"You look after your dad, little guy." Shane gave Luke a little high five before wandering over to his brother.

While Helena and Gráinne said their umpteenth goodbye, it was the brothers turn to do the same.

Darren kept rubbing the back of his neck as he walked towards his brother, his steps heavy and jaunted. Shane was the opposite, his shoulders hunched under the weight of what he was about to do. Both were dreading this moment in their own way.

I knew this would hurt Darren, but he had me and his friends to pick him up. Shane was not only losing his brother and his family, he was also losing his pack and everything he had ever known. Although Darren would have to explain the truth to their father. I wasn't sure who had the raw deal there.

Darren flung an arm around his younger brother's shoulder, pulling him into an embrace so tight Shane winced. They stood in silence, hugging tightly before Shane found his voice.

"I'm not sure I can do this." Shane buried his face in his brother's shoulder.

"You can. You have a baby on the way, it's time to man up." Darren replied, trying to keep his tone gruff, but emotion clouded his every word.

Their words carried towards me in the wind.

Shane nodded, staring towards the ferry with wide, fearful eyes.

They stood like that for some time, making promises and adding words of encouragement on both sides. When Shane beckoned for Gráinne to join them, Helena and I turned away to give them some privacy, but I could tell by the way she was watching me, she knew I could hear every word of their conversation.

The loud foghorn blared in a final warning. I quickly covered Luke's ears before he would start crying again. Shane and Gráinne shared a look and simultaneously gulped. We all made towards the pier for their final goodbyes, but another sound of the horn warned us they were running out of time.

"Take care of your family little bro." Darren's hand lingered as he placed the keys into Shane's before pulling him in for one last hug.

Shane bit back tears, at a loss for words. Darren finally released him, practically shoving his brother away before stepping backwards to stand in line with me and Luke.

Helena wiped her friend's cheeks and gave her another embrace before patting her shoulders like a mother would. "You ring me when you get settled in, alright?"

Gráinne nodded and retreated to Shane's side. He took her hand and their shoulders rose as they took a deep breath before getting into the rental car they would swap out once the ferry docked, marking the start of their new life. Throwing one last glance backwards and waving, Shane edged the car forwards in the queue boarding until they disappeared into the ferry hold.

I glanced at Darren, catching him wiping his cheeks with his sleeves.

"They'll be okay," I said softly, giving my friend a gentle pat on the back while pulling a sniffling Helena into my side. "We all will."

He nodded, his jaw twitching. "Dad is going to kill me. Once for running off after the funeral, and twice for letting Shane go."

I knew their dad well. He was a lovely man full of laughter and light. Their parents wouldn't be angry, maybe hurt they had been left out, but they would understand why we had to save Shane and their grandchild, especially when we exposed the truth about Damien.

"Boad!" Luke squealed, interrupting the moment to point at the ferry now pulling away from the dock.

Shane and Gráinne stood on the deck, leaning over the railing with one arm around each other as they waved and said goodbye to their home.

<h1 style="text-align:center">CHAPTER 29</h1>

The drive home had been long and silent. I didn't have the right words. Darren had lost a brother; Helena had said goodbye to her best friend. my heart was heavy in an entirely different way. I wasn't just going to have to say goodbye to my family, I had to kill someone who had been like a brother to me growing up. Yes, we never got along, and he was a murderer who needed to be stopped for the good of my pack, but I'd be lying if I said I didn't feel any guilt.

Darren's voice drifted in from the hallway. He was on the phone to Mary, running through the plan one last time, but there was an impatience and shortness to his tone that gave away the truth. There was no need for twenty questions or grilling her on the plan, she would text when the hunt began. But Darren was a general on a mission now that his brother's safety was out of his hands, and he wouldn't rest until he knew everything was in order.

With Luke tucked into his make-shift bed on the couch, it left only me and Helena in the kitchen. She pottered around, her touch light but shaky as she moved from one end of the room to the other tidying and fussing.

I reached out as a plate slipped from her hand and was well on its way to smashing into pieces if it hadn't been for my quick reflexes.

"Sorry." Helena winced, balling her hand into a fist and pressing it to her forehead as if it might stop the tears she was trying to bite back.

"You have nothing to apologise for." I placed the plate safely back on the drying rack before winding my arms around her waist and pulling her close. "Nothing at all."

She slumped into my embrace, her cheeks flushed and the tell-tale hiccup coming before she burst into tears. "I'm a mess."

I placed my finger and thumb under her chin, tilting her head up. "You are a chaotic ball of energy at the best of times, but not a mess. You have more strength in your little finger than I have in my whole body."

"I'm not that strong." Helena shook her head, wiping furiously at her eyes.

"Yes, you are," I murmured, staring intently into her emerald eyes which had captured my heart. "My pack is falling apart, I brought my son back to a bloodbath, and I'm a failure as a father. When my world started splitting at the seams, I came to you. You helped us come up with a plan. So, tell me how I'm the strong one?"

She ignored my question, leaning into my touch. "You're not a failure, you're an amazing father."

When I didn't interrupt, she studied my face carefully.

"You're not responsible for your father's misgivings, or your brother's actions," she whispered, and I found myself wondering not for the first time if she could see into my soul.

I pulled her closer, finding comfort in the heat of her body pressed against mine, gently kissing the top of her head before leaning my forehead against hers. "Thanks. I think I needed to hear that."

She simply smiled and stared up at me with a look that gave me more confidence and encouragement than I could muster myself.

"What if..." I began, but she reached up and pressed her index finger against my lips to silence my spiralling thoughts.

"Do you really think I would let you do this if I thought I could lose you?" She traced her finger across the curve of my lips to stroke my cheek. "If you can avoid fighting him, do, but if it comes to it, I understand you need to protect your son and your pack."

I was scared—terrified. If this went wrong, Luke could lose me. After Laura passed, I'd cared little for my life and would have happily walked in front of a bus if it hadn't been for my son. Now here I was, risking him growing up an orphan, but if I didn't stop Damien, Luke would be in danger anyway. Damien was ruthless and would stop at nothing to keep his power.

"I'm just scared this will backfire," I said finally, gently nuzzling her cheek.

"You can't force everyone to listen to you but showing the pack the truth and allowing them to make their own choice is the only way forwards."

I closed my eyes, willing my problems away. "And if they don't leave?"

"Then they're not your family or your pack. They don't share the same values or want the same kind of future," she said, keeping her gaze firmly fixed on mine. "You do what you have to do."

"I really wish our life was more normal," I muttered, gently rocking back and forth while keeping one ear on the baby monitor as Luke mooched about in his sleep.

Helena shrugged, a wry smile playing on her lips. "Normal wouldn't cut it for me. That's why I fell for you."

Her words brought my attention straight back to her.

"I love you." I slid one hand up her back to rest against the nape of her neck, nerves exploding into butterflies in my stomach as the truth hung in the air between us.

"I love you too," she replied, her voice thick with emotion.

Staring down at her beautiful cat-like eyes, the freckles dusting her cheeks, I couldn't understand why I'd been granted a second chance at love.

She smiled and leaned up on her tiptoes to brush her lips across mine. "Everything will be alright, I promise."

Lost in her eyes, the noise of Darren pacing in the hallway faded into the background, and I forgot where I was. I wanted to forget everything. I pulled her close and crushed my lips against hers as if her kiss might save me from the nightmare we both lived in.

My sanctuary was short lived as the kitchen door was flung open and banged into the counter.

Darren strode through, his serious expression replaced by an eye roll as he took in the image of me and Helena entangled before turning sour again.

"I hate to break up the moment, but it's time."

CHAPTER 30

We pulled into a side entrance on the outskirts of the forest. On this the side of the mountain, we were downwind from the manor but close to where the pack would gather to begin their hunt. It ensured Damien wouldn't know we were coming, and the trees lining the edge of the boreen hid our cars well. If anyone passed by, they wouldn't notice. A supermoon peaked over the crest of the mountain and obscured by a thin veil of clouds, it was a stark reminder we were running out of time. The foggy night sky and the condensation on the car window coupled with the enormity of what we were about to do gave the night an all too sinister feeling. The place I first changed, the forest I ran in with my pack for years, it didn't feel like home anymore.

"You ready?" Darren asked, rubbing his hands together to ward off the bite of the cold summer's night.

I shrugged, my trainers sinking into the bark lined trail as we started our descend into the forest. "Nope, but we have to do this."

The forest felt heavy, as if the canopy was weighing down on me. I focused on putting one foot in front of the other, trying to keep my mind off Mary. I wasn't pleased with her decision to stay with the pack, but I understood she wanted to stay for the funeral and felt some kind of moral obligation to be there to guard her pack. Even so, I couldn't help but worry. She was feisty and stubborn, fantastic traits that made her a force to be reckoned with, but she had lost her calm demeanour, and I wasn't sure I trusted her decision making abilities at the moment. What if she blew up at Damien? What if he hurt her? Living alongside the man who murdered your family was no small task.

We walked in silence for a few minutes before Darren's nerves got the better of him, and his mouth went into overdrive.

"So, how is this going to play out?" He scuffed the loamy turf with his foot, sending a stick skittering into the bushy undergrowth.

"Mary has the real death cert, the police report, and a witness statement showing Damien at the scene of the crime. He has motive. We have the letters from her father saying they were in danger." I rolled my shoulders in an attempt to relieve the tension knotting them. "I'm hoping my father will back us."

Darren scoffed before shooting me an apologetic look. "Sorry, but I can't see your dad stepping in. He let you leave."

"The proof we have makes them both look guilty. If he wants to save his skin and his own reputation, he has to."

"Banking on his pride? That's gutsy," he mused.

I sighed, rubbing my forehead with the palm of my hand. "It's all he has left. He's not the alpha, and it doesn't look like he's in control of the situation. He might not care about me, but Luke is his family legacy. He'd never want him to leave."

He shook his head. "Luke is your legacy, not your family's."

"Thanks," I said, the faintest hint of a smile ghosting my lips. "If anything happens…"

Darren held his hand up to silence me. "Don't. Your family is mine."

I nodded and we both lapsed into silence. Neither of us mentioned the possibility of this ending in another bloodbath. I wanted to avoid a fight to the death if I could, though my gut told me Damien was dying for one.

Darren's phone buzzed in his pocket, almost on queue.

"It's Mary," he said, the dull green light of his phone screen illuminating his worried face. "She says they're at the clearing. We need to hurry."

No longer in the mood to talk, Darren picked up the pace and strayed off the main path.

I sprinted after him, following as he led the way through the undergrowth. It would have been faster to shift, but I didn't want this confirmation to turn physical. Turning up in our wolf forms to crash the hunt would give Damien the perfect excuse to start a fight. Plus, wolf communication really wasn't enough to get our point across in this situation.

It was frustrating though. Even with my superhuman reflexes, every time a twig snapped loudly or the ground beneath my feet gave way and my ankle rolled, the magic surging through my veins begged me to change.

Not yet.

For some time, the only noise was the sound of the breeze as it whipped through the trees, the leaves and twigs crunching beneath our feet, and the sound of our heavy breathing as we kept up the pace. We couldn't risk getting there after the hunt had begun. I had no doubt Damien wouldn't hesitate to kill either of us if he got the chance. Picking us off one by one on the side would be just his style. Eventually, another noise rose, the gentle hum of voices in the distance.

I could smell them, the familiar scent of the pack members

all gathered together. Because we were downwind, they couldn't smell us coming. When we were closer, Darren slowed, and we stopped about 20 feet away, hiding behind a thick tree trunk.

Peering around the side of the tree, I could see them gathered in the clearing.

"So, when do we crash the party?" Darren asked, his chest rising and falling as he panted slightly.

I shook my head, retreating back behind the tree. "Not yet. Let Damien start with one of his Hitler speeches and then we'll step in. I don't want him to claim some sort of ambush —this has to be done right."

Any human would have been exhausted after running the distance we did, but we had just worked up a light sweat. Being a werewolf had its perks.

"I'm not sure if accusing a prospective alpha of murder can be done right," Darren muttered.

We ran over the plan again while the pack was chatting away, but once their volume levels began to dip, we fell silent. They couldn't hear us over the thrum of their conversation, but once the blanket of silence fell, we were within hearing range.

As the crowd hushed, Damien's voice came into the fore, echoing throughout the forest.

"First, let me begin by thanking you all for gathering here tonight. The last few months have been impossibly difficult—losing our alpha was a huge blow. I cannot even begin to fathom how difficult this must have been for his children."

From our vantage point, I could just see the top of Damien's head in the centre of the clearing. Another slightly taller figure stood beside him with straight shoulders and a piercing cold gaze. I couldn't pick Mary out in the crowd, but I could imagine how much Damien's words were raising her hackles. I silently willed her to hold it together until the right time, despite my blood boiling too.

"Losing Cormac was a horrible loss, but his poor tortured soul is now at rest," Damien continued, his tone dripping with false empathy. His words were empty and cold, just like his heart.

Darren gave me a nudge, and we started edging closer to the clearing, keeping our bodies low and our steps light as we snuck through the undergrowth. The soil in this area of the forest was soft and loamy due to the nearby river, helping us mask our movements.

"We must continue to pull together and rebuild. Our pack is a family, and we must show our strength and resilience in the face of such adversity." He shot a pointed look in one direction that must have been where Mary was standing. "We need to stop casting silly assumptions and fighting among ourselves."

It took all my self-control not to snort at that.

"I took this position on the basis that Cormac would one day follow in his father's footsteps..."

As Damien droned on, we crept closer until we were on the fringes of the clearing. As the breeze blew, Damien's head snapped up and he zeroed in on our direction.

"Shit." Darren cursed, ducking back behind a tree as if we could hide again.

Mary was supposed to give us another signal to let us know if Larissa was there, but I was ready. I knew we couldn't get that close without being caught. This was a werewolf pack after all, not some social gathering.

Throwing my shoulders back, I strode forwards, leaving the cover shadows as I stepped out into the clearing. A chorus of gasps arose, and the pack members nearby turned to face me. I caught sight of Mary standing to my right, arms folded, one hip cocked out like she was ready to tear someone apart both verbally and physically. Our eyes met and she smiled, but it didn't quite reach her eyes, which were burning with a lust for revenge.

"What are you doing here?" Damien's demanding tone ripped through the crowd.

"We had a date, did we not?" I quipped with a shrug, surprising myself with my laid-back approach. "I'm here to talk to my pack, to tell them the truth."

Damien's face went from pink to a dark shade of red, his mouth contorting in a nasty scowl.

Not waiting for an invitation, I walked through the pack until I was in the centre of the clearing and stopped far enough from Damien so he wasn't within punching range— for his sake as much as mine.

As much as I tried to avoid his gaze, I caught sight of my father in the corner of my eye. Instead of wearing a look of disapproval, he was intrigued.

What did he think this was? Me stepping up and fighting to be alpha instead so I could be a part of his master plan? No, this is about the truth.

"Get off the pack lands, now," Damien ordered, throwing his hands in the air like a temperamental child.

I shook my head, a wry smile playing on my lips. "Not this time. I'm not playing your games anymore."

CHAPTER 31

A low growl rattled in Damien's throat, but I paid him no heed. Instead, I turned my back to him and faced my pack, my family. My confidence began to waver when I noticed the confusion on their faces, some even stretching to mistrust, but I couldn't stop. I had to hope they would believe me.

"I'm here to tell you that our alpha wasn't killed in that car accident. He was murdered."

Whispers rippled through the pack at my revelation. Wide eyes stared at me in disbelief. Darren had stepped into line with Mary, and both of them gave me an encouraging nod, but I could tell by the way Darren's shoulders tensed he wasn't too sure how this would play out either.

It was my father who stepped forwards, pressing a protective arm across Damien's chest to stop him from launching himself at me.

"What are you talking about?" he demanded, the authority in his voice unmistakable.

Maybe he is the puppet master.

"Damien killed our alpha. He ran them off the road and

killed Luke and his wife in cold blood," I said, turning to glare at my father. "And you helped him."

My father paled a fraction, and his eyes narrowed. "I did no such thing."

Damn, it felt good twisting that knife.

"This is ridiculous," Damien finally piped up, shoving my father's arm away. "You have no right coming here and slandering my good name. I know you chose the doctor route, but we have a law firm that will bury you if I don't rip you apart first."

I stepped forwards so that we were toe-to-toe, a knowing smirk twisting my lips as I taunted him. "Try me. I dare you."

"You have no proof, only hearsay," Damien snapped, pulling away to face his pack, putting on his best politician mask. "This is an absolute farce, bitter jealousy. Please, don't listen to anymore nonsense."

Some looked to me for more information, others looked to Damien for leadership. Maybe they had been through too much. Perhaps losing our alpha had left too much uncertainty for them to cope with. Having no alpha made our pack vulnerable, but it was no excuse for turning a blind eye to this.

Mary stepped forwards, slapping a brown envelope in my hands. How she'd managed to hide it on the way to the hunt, I had no idea. She was as cunning as Damien, and now it was her turn for revenge.

"You killed my parents." Mary squared up to Damien. Despite being half his size, claws protruded from her fingertips, and she looked ready to kill. "You took my family from me, my brother. You're no alpha."

Damien's mask slipped when his eyes flashed with anger. He opened his mouth, but then bit his tongue and smoothed his expression when he remembered his audience. "You've been through so much, Mary. You're not thinking straight."

I ground my jaw at his condescending tone.

"I'm thinking clearer than ever," she snapped, grabbing two sheets of paper from the envelope and holding it high in the air as she turned to address the pack. "This is the death certificate, the real one that states that the cause of death was not trauma from the car crash, but from having their hearts torn out. The autopsy completed by a human doctor says the same."

"Humans know nothing," my father snorted through gritted teeth.

Damien shook his head with a dismissive hand. "I've never seen this death certificate before. The one on pack records states they died in the car crash."

"So you're saying you never knew my father falsified the cert?" I chimed in, locking eyes with Damien.

He hesitated before choosing his words carefully, avoiding eye contact with my father. "I am as shocked as the rest of us. I presumed the alpha died in the crash as per the official reports. I had no reason to believe there was foul play."

My father turned to glower at his beloved *son*, his eyes flashing silver when he realised Damien would throw him under the bus to save his own skin.

I couldn't help feeling a small sense of satisfaction seeing my father's plans crumbling before him.

"Funny that." Mary waved the paper in his face. "Because I went back to speak to the police again, and once I had a witch remove the spell twisting his memory of that night, he said you were at the scene with blood on your hands."

Damien's upper lip curled back. "Lies."

"So, the Garda first on the scene lied about seeing you?" I pressed, pulling out the signed statement Niamh had given us, along with the voice recorder. "A werewolf wouldn't die in a car crash unless the tree impaled them both perfectly in the heart, yet Mary saw them before the burial and that story didn't add up. We all saw them on the pyre. Oh, and not to mention the warning the alpha left his children."

"You're making all of this up."

Damien's eyes narrowed. My father looked absolutely disgusted with the scene unfolding before him.

"My dad left me a letter warning that someone was trying to kill him, and he warned us Cormac would be next," Mary explained, emotion filling her words as she pointed a damning finger in Damien's direction. "You gave my brother nightshade and staged it to look like suicide."

I wasn't sure how his twisted mind worked, but I was pretty sure Damien was looking for an escape plan. He schooled his expression into one of feigned innocence with a hint of outrage. He'd always been a good actor.

Damien shook his head, raising his voice and spreading his arms while addressing the pack. "I did no such thing. Whatever Fiachra has done, I was not aware of any of this."

My father looked like he was about to swing for him, but Damien shot him a warning look to stay quiet, as if to say he was going to fix this mess.

"Yes, you did. Both of you conspired to kill our alpha so that you could take over the pack. You even went after my son when we found out the truth." My confidence grew as a murmur of unease swept through the crowd. Turning to Damien, I hammered the final nail in his coffin and clicked play on the voice recorder.

"You're creating conspiracies where there are none. I wasn't anywhere near the alpha on the night of his death. Larissa can vouch that I was with her." Damien stood tall, speaking as loud as he could to stop the pack from hearing the recording clearly.

I scoffed. "That witch's word means nothing, especially when she was at the scene too."

The moment the words left my mouth, the recording cut

out, and I felt the tug of magic as the voice recorder escaped my grasp, vanishing into thin air.

"It's a pity you have such a low opinion of me."

Larissa stepped out of the shadows, dressed in a floor-length black dress and a long cloak that trailed behind her, bright red to match her lips. The pack members nearby tripped over themselves in their hurry to part the circle and allow her through. She strode into the centre of the clearing, fixing me with that stone-cold stare of hers as she toyed with the voice recorder.

Any faux confidence I had felt up until that point evaporated.

"Cat got your tongue?" She teased, her eyes lighting up with amusement.

Damien looked as worried as me for some reason, shifting nervously from foot to foot.

When she couldn't get a reaction from me, Larissa zeroed in on Damien. "What exactly is going on here? I came to name you as the next alpha, yet here is your contender. You claimed he forfeited his right."

"Cormac is dead, his nomination no longer stands." My father's tone cooled as he looked towards the coward he'd called son.

Was he still seriously pushing for Damien after he threw him under the bus so easily?

The faintest lines creased her forehead, and she shot Damien a look of displeasure. "No, the nomination still stands. I thought I made that point clear, but obviously, sending a mutt to do a woman's job was a mistake."

Her words made my blood run cold.

Cormac wasn't supposed to die, it had been meant to be me. But Damien was a coward and Cormac was easy prey.

For the first time in a long time, my father appeared genuinely shocked. He looked from Larissa to Damien, and judging by the look on his face, they'd gone behind his back.

"How could you betray me? After everything I did for you," my father snapped, his voice booming throughout the clearing without a care for whom heard him. "This was your plan, not mine. I would never have agreed to that."

Larissa clucked her tongue impatiently. "Fiachra, it's not personal."

"My family *is* personal." He growled, turning to Damien with disgust. "I warned you to back off after the bracelet."

Damien paused as if considering his options, surveying the pack as they looked on in a mixture of stunned silence and fear. I think it was then he decided to use fear rather than continue playing his part.

"Fiachra, why did you do it? Because Luke let the witches kill my father all those years ago?" Damien asked, not giving my father a chance to answer before continuing. "You blamed him for your wife's death too. Did years of hatred and loneliness drive you to do this?"

"This plan was of your making, and I warned you not to go through with it," my father spat, slapping his hand away. "I should never have helped cover your tracks. I was a fool to think you would ever be able to lead the pack. Patrick would be turning in his grave if he had one."

Instead of losing his temper, Damien actually smirked, fire and ice dancing in his eyes as he stared at my father. "My father would be proud."

"Enough," I said, grabbing the papers from Mary. "You can't pin all of this on my father."

"I agree," Larissa chimed in, her cloak swirling as she threw out one hand towards my father, her fingers flexed. "I've had quite enough of this."

He froze in place, his hands dropping to his sides, bound by an invisible force of magic I could feel radiating in the air.

My father stiffened, and a low growl rumbled in his throat, fists clenched at his side. "I didn't do it, and I can prove it beyond doubt."

"End this, now," Larissa demanded, her steely gaze fixed on my father. "Or I will."

I jumped forwards on pure instinct, but I was too late.

Before I could reach them, Damien launched into action and threw my father to the ground. In one swift movement, he smashed his fist through my father's ribcage and ripped his heart out.

CHAPTER 32

As I crashed into Damien, we tumbled to the ground, a twisted mass of contorted limbs and snapping bones as we shifted simultaneously. A cloud of magic expanded and settled over the clearing. This was the most painful transition I'd experienced since my teenage years, shifting without the ground beneath my feet or any sense of control had a primal fire to it that set my temper alight. My body felt threatened, and fuelled by anger and the need for revenge, my magical side responded in kind.

The transition allowed me to untangle myself from our contact and jump back. When the dust settled, we were facing one another, both crouching with our bellies low to the ground.

Whispers quickly grew into full blown chaos as the pack reacted. I could hear the unmistakable cackle of Larissa as she watched on with pure glee.

"Tom!" Mary's shrill voice rang out, slicing through the chaos.

All around us, the noise levels surged along with the magic. They could all feel the pull, but no one else stepped into the fight. When a wolf challenges for the role of alpha, they're on their own.

Damien was watching me, his black coat glossy under the moonlight, and I swore he had grown at least a foot since I'd last fought him.

No, he didn't grow, the damn witch is helping him.

When a new alpha was inducted in allegiance with the witches, they bestowed powers upon them. I'd never understood how it worked; those were secrets reserved for the alpha alone, but every alpha had always seemed extra strong, as if they'd locked into a higher power. History books claimed only the worthy could step up to the mark, but Damien had proven that wrong. Somehow, she was helping him anyway. He was like some kind of Disney villain come to life, but there was nothing magical about him. Only darkness shone in those empty eyes of his. He cared for nothing but power, and I wasn't going to let him get away with it.

Damien took one step towards me, his new improved frame hulking over me by half a foot. Drool dripped from his lips as they curled back, and he snarled, flashing me a glimpse of his fangs.

Two could play that game. I wasn't going to be intimidated, so I planted my paws firmly on the ground and locked my shoulder blades as I rose to my full height, baring my canines in response.

The full moon illuminated the clearing, but my razor-sharp eyesight didn't need it. I could see each movement Damien made, noticed every ripple of muscle.

Our stare down lasted for what seemed like forever. I wanted to take him on, every instinct in my body screamed for me to go for his throat, but I'd sworn I wasn't going to fight. Yet here I was, as if he was ever going to let me tell the truth and take it lying down.

The slightest twitch of Damien's tail gave him away.

I dug the claws of my back legs into the soft turf, sat back on my haunches and sprang at Damien just as he went for me. Instead of clashing head on, I twisted my body in the air to avoid his snapping jaws and lashed out with my front claws, catching his shoulder as we collided.

Damien yelped, and the sound sent a thrilling shiver down my spine. I landed with a light thud and immediately spun to see him land off kilter. His right side faltered as he hit the ground, and he recoiled and turned on me with a look of absolute hatred.

I was the one thing standing in his way, and he had every intention of going through me.

While my own bloodlust was surging, I had one constant reminder keeping me grounded. They say you can lose your human side when the red mist descends, but there was something about the blood bond I had with my son that overrode that. Despite my body begging me to give in, he kept me tied to reality. I couldn't leave him orphaned.

Despite me getting the first blow in, Damien recovered and made his next move. He came at me again, this time sprinting full force in my direction rather than taking another giant leap. The time for theatrics was apparently over.

I dodged to the side once or twice before I realised the hard way that playing a game of cat and mouse wasn't going to work for me. He caught my left flank as I tried to dodge another charge, and a low growl ripped from my chest in protest. It stung like hell and forced me off balance as I twisted around and returned the favour.

Damien wasn't only bigger, he was faster. Whatever that witch had done had turbo charged his rage.

He danced back, blood dripping from his fangs as he snarled in return and charged again.

Instead of running, I faced him head on, a chorus of howls

and clashing teeth echoing as we tried to overpower each other, but his aim and tactics were never as good as mine.

When we untangled ourselves and darted back, a pool of blood dripped onto the ground in front of me. We were both covered in bites, and blood coated our fur. A flap of skin torn open on Damien's neck oozed blood, and the satisfaction briefly helped numb the pain coursing through my body.

He went down, and a screeching howl ripped from his lips.

The clearing fell silent.

Damien's chest rose and fell with heavy breaths, but he didn't move.

I padded forwards slowly, wincing at each movement and inhaled deeply. The potent scent of blood and sweat filled my nostrils.

Still, Damien didn't move. I could hear a pulse, his heart still beating erratically, but his eyes were closed and his body limp, too wounded to get to his feet.

A new feeling surged through me, elation at winning the fight I never wanted. I turned to face the pack, seeing concern etched into my friend's features. I couldn't believe it was over.

Just as I was about to shift, something hard slammed into my back.

My legs gave way and my claws sliced through the turf as I slid forwards with the force. A flash of pain jolted through my back, and I howled, though it came out more like a screech. Stars danced in my vision.

I smelled him all over me, heard his panting, and felt my blood mixed with drool dripping on me as Damien clamped his jaw around my neck. He didn't even have the decency to come from me head on. Always a coward.

Luke's face flashed through my mind and guilt and anguish hit me like a ten-tonne wave.

Trapped under Damien's weight, I howled again as his canines bit into my skin.

CHAPTER 33

All I could think of was Luke, see those innocent hazel eyes of his, and then I heard a voice like an angel coaxing me back to life, telling me not give up.

Laura.

The voice grew stronger, less subtle, and more determined and encouraging. Pain coursed through my body, and I felt my energy slipping away as time slowed down.

Get up.

Fight back.

I heard Luke's laugh. I saw his playful smile in my mind, feel his little hand in mine. I remembered the kaleidoscope of emotions I felt the first time I held my son in my arms.

Don't give up.

Something clicked in me and time swung back into action. I was pinned to the ground, and Damien's teeth were digging into my windpipe while I lay gasping for air. I scrambled to brace my hind legs beneath me and pushed with every ounce of strength I had left to buck my legs and flip my body over, throwing Damien off in the process. Fresh pain seared through me as his teeth ripped from my skin and we both flipped and landed with a loud thud on the ground.

I pushed through the pain, forcing my shaking legs into motion. Before I could dive on Damien, a brown blur of fur rushed forwards and smashed into him.

At first, I thought it was Darren, but then I saw him darting towards the fight from the side-lines alone.

Mary.

Guilt swept over me, and a new sense of purpose thrummed through my veins. The sight of my friends fighting Damien, breaking the rules to save me, made me realise this wasn't just about revenge or exposing the truth. We had to save the pack. I couldn't let Luke lose me, but I also wouldn't let my friends fight this battle for me. This was my family's mess and I would end it.

I watched in horror as Damien turned on Mary, snapping at her hind legs and throwing her off balance long enough to flip her onto her back. She fought against him, claws slashing at his chest, and she sank her teeth into his shoulder. He snarled in disgust and drew one leg back to smack her across the muzzle. She whimpered but continued to thrash, trapped under his larger form.

Damien threw his head back, his extended canines glinting under the light of the full moon as he readied a killer blow.

Something snapped deep inside me, and the magic that normally felt like the swell of the sea crested and burst into a multitude of colours, tingling all the way from my toes to my muzzle. I launched off the ground, clearing several feet in record time, and I slammed into Damien, knocking him off Mary and burying him into the ground back first.

He let out a howl of agony, eyes widening at the shock of the impact.

Darren was seconds behind me, kneeling by Mary and

murmuring words of comfort as he tended to whatever damage Damien had done.

Seeing my friend in pain only fuelled my anger. While I kept Damien pinned there, I realised it was taking far less effort than it should. We no longer felt so mismatched. It was like the old days when I'd kicked his ass, and he'd had to tap out. But this time, I didn't want to let him go.

Damien squirmed in my grip, but I kept one paw on his chest and my jaw clamped around his throat. He thrashed and kicked at my stomach. I returned in kind, ignoring the scratches and bruises covering my body.

The fear in his eyes gave me a sick thrill I had never expected to feel. He grew weaker as I increased the pressure on his throat.

Larissa stood to one side, her brow furrowed in deep concentration, and her lips pressed in a thin line as she struggled to give Damien more power. As his life force slipped away bit by bit, their connection severed.

The pack watched the scene unfold, holding their breath or crying, some even hiding behind one another. No one stepped in to stop me though, no one tried to save their new 'Alpha'. He'd killed the only person who might have saved him.

Damien was alone.

Luke's innocent little face popped into my mind again as I saw two kids cowering behind their mother. It was then I realised I wasn't a killer. I came here to give the pack a choice, and I would honour that promise.

I retracted my teeth from Damien's throat, bloody saliva dripping from my mouth as I slowly released my grip on him entirely and stepped back. He was covered in wounds, just like me, but he looked the worst for it. The look of defeat and anger on his face said it all. I was showing mercy, and he had no choice but to accept it.

Darren rushed forwards to stand over Damien with his legs shoulder width apart and arms folded like a bodyguard, giving him another incentive not to try for another round.

I gingerly rose to my feet and shifted back into my human form, relishing in the feeling as my magic washed over my body. The shift hurt and stung as my injuries jarred the transition, but something was pumping through my veins, and it wasn't just adrenaline. Even in my human form, everything was that bit sharper, clearer. It was like the first time I shifted into wolf form and back, but I felt stronger.

It was only when I was standing naked among them that I realised just how quiet the pack had become. Any disagreements or protests had stopped. The fight was over. Damien was slowly picking himself off the ground, having shifted back too. The noise erupted once more.

Larissa stalked over to Damien with a face like thunder, shoving him straight off his feet. "You're no alpha."

Ignoring them, I walked over to check on Mary, who was wrapped in someone else's jacket. I thought she was crying, but I soon noticed the blood-soaked tissue in her hands and realised she was covering her face for an entirely different reason.

"Let me see," I murmured, crouching in front of her, gently reaching out to touch her shoulder as not to startle her.

Mary peeked over her fingertips and lowered her shaking hands to reveal a deep laceration from her left cheekbone to the corner of her lips. It wasn't a clean cut and it was healing too slowly, I could smell wolfsbane on her breath. The bastard must have tried to weaken her before the ceremony. The jagged edge and raw skin around the wound told me this would never heal cleanly, but I wasn't going to tell her that now.

"Let's go get you cleaned up, and I'll have a look at that

cut." I slipped straight into doctor mode, wiping a tear off the bridge of her nose.

She shook her head, the movement making her wince. "No, you have something to do first."

"What? No, I'm treating you now."

"No, you're sorting this pack out," Mary said firmly, nudging me back towards Darren. "You came here to fix this mess. I'm not leaving until it's sorted, and neither are you. You have a job to do now."

I frowned, not quite sure what she meant with the last part. I hadn't beaten Damien.

"Go," Mary insisted, shoving me away.

I reluctantly hauled my stiff body to my feet and walked back over to Darren.

"Here." He thrust an oversized hoodie into my hands along with a pair of jeans. "Put these on."

Darren rolled his eyes at my confusion. "Hurry up, you need to look the part."

Only then did I notice Darren was in his boxers and these were his clothes, but I didn't argue. The pack was deep in discussion around us, but I was still in the centre of the clearing stark naked, and I wasn't too keen on addressing them when they were all clothed. It was like the reverse of what you imagine in interviews.

Once dressed, I made a beeline for Damien. He was on his knees before Larissa, his pleading growing louder as he saw me approach.

"He'll never—" Damien began, but he was cut off by a swift kick to the face.

Larissa wiped the blood off the toe of her shoe on the grass, giving Damien a look of utter disdain before her attention shifted to me. "I can't induct you as the new alpha of the Faolchúnna pack unless you finish the job."

"I don't want to be the alpha of this pack. What it once

stood for, any history or integrity it once held is gone. I won't murder for a seat at the table."

The witch cocked her head to one side, studying me like I was a mouse that both irritated and surprised her.

"Everyone." I cleared my throat to get the pack's attention. I expected to have more difficulty, but their gaze had never left us and silence quickly fell. "I didn't come here to fight tonight; I came to tell you the truth. You deserved to know what happened to our alpha, Luke, and what your so-called new alpha was, a murderer."

A soft murmur travelled through the pack.

"He murdered Mary's parents and then Cormac, all in his desperate quest for power."

"So what? This pack needed more power, the world is changing rapidly," Damien interjected, slowly rising to his feet. "We need to change with it."

"We were changing," I snapped, anger boiling in my core once more. "You murdered in cold blood, for what? Power."

He scowled. "The old rules are archaic. The pack should be able to elect their alpha and not rely on blood right."

"I agree, but you're the one trying to claim some skewed blood-right and look what that's done." My voice cracked slightly as the gravity of what happened began to hit.

"Cormac was never going to be a great leader. We needed someone willing to make strong decisions with a vision for our future where our pack is self-sufficient and will not be challenged." Damien looked to the crowd for support in desperation. He caught sight of my father's dead body and turned a light shade of green.

I should have snapped his neck.

I still could.

Darren placed a heavy hand on my shoulder as if reading my mind.

"A pack that is only about power and status, that will

murder in cold blood to get what they want is not one I want to be part of. That's not what I stand for and not what I want my son to grow up in." I surveyed the pack as I spoke, taking in their mixed reactions. "A pack is about family, tradition, loving and supporting one another through this changing world and finding a way to live among humans, not under the thumb of the witches."

"This isn't my pack either." Darren walked over to join my side. "I'm with Tom."

Wait what?

"You know rogues don't survive long, right?" Damien sneered, rolling his eyes.

"They're not talking about rogues—they're talking about a new pack," Mary said, her voice thick with emotion.

I swallowed hard. I wasn't sure I was ready for his. I was hardly the man for the job—I was too young. Yet the magic inside me answered the call. I could feel the pull. But an alpha needed a witch's blessing to lead...*Or did they?*

"I know you can feel it." Darren shot Damien a smug smirk. "Tom is an alpha. He was born to lead, unlike you."

Larissa rolled her eyes and looked between Damien and me with a resigned sigh. "What are you saying, Tom?"

"I'm leaving the pack, and I want to give everyone here a choice," I explained, sounding more confident than I felt. "I won't kill him, so Damien has the right to be alpha. Either the pack can stay with you or stand with me, it's their choice."

"Go where? You have nothing."

Mary stepped in, shooting him the darkest of looks. "The second house in Kildare, it's Tom's now."

"Absolutely not!" Damien spluttered in dismay.

"I could have killed you, taken this pack for my own by force." I warned, squaring up to him. "I'm not asking."

Damien's face was beetroot under the myriad of bruises and cuts.

"It's yours," Larissa cut in, raising a hand to silence the crowd and a seething Damien. "I decree that Tom Whelan has the right to leave the Faolchúnna pack."

"I appreciate that, but I don't need your permission."

She was just as much responsible for everything as Damien was. He may have ripped my father's heart out, but it was on her orders. If anything, she was the real puppeteer.

"Anyone who wants to join Tom's pack, please step forwards." Larissa ignored my bitter remark, her tone growing bored. She didn't even wait to see who joined, storming back over to Damien to give him a thick ear. "You better not make me regret this alliance."

I held my breath when it looked like no one was going to move, but then one of Mary's friends stepped forwards, followed by another. Aoife and her family stepped forwards, and she shot me a small smile of encouragement. By the end, about one third of the pack had stepped forwards. The others who hung back had family connections high up in the law firm. Whatever kept them back, be it fear or greed, they weren't the type of person I wanted in my pack.

I looked around at the pack members that had chosen me, that believed in *me*. Tears clogged my throat as I whispered. "Thank you."

Damien turned to us, spitting his words through gritted teeth. "You have an hour to gather your things and then you are not welcome on pack lands again."

Just like that, I was an alpha.

EPILOGUE

When you grow up in a werewolf pack, you often wonder what it's like to be alpha. Most boys dream of it, and I'd be lying if I said I wasn't one of them. But I never knew how satisfying it would be to watch my own pack grow and come to life. It had been a year since the pack split, and while it had been tough, things were finally coming together.

As I stood in front of a large house with slate-grey brickwork nestled between a forest and a wide expanse of meadows that stretched for miles, I couldn't help but smile. The Faolchúnna pack bought the property years ago for expansion. It had no history of bloodshed and betrayal, it was home. Nestled in the midlands, it was the perfect place to start our new pack.

"I can't believe this is our home," I marvelled, unable to stop the smile playing on my lips as I watched Luke run around the grassy area in front of the house with some other kids.

Helena's smile mirrored my own as she wrapped an arm around my waist. "It's perfect."

The roar of an engine broke the peace and Darren's car

quickly came into view, the tyres leaving a puff of dust in their wake as he sped along the gravelled drive and screeched to a stop in front of the house. Luke squealed and ran towards the car, but Helena was over like a shot and scooped him into her arms before he could get into danger.

Darren stepped out and ruffled Luke's hair before beginning to unpack bags from the trunk.

Months later and we were still slowly moving everyone's things from the Faolchúnna pack lands. There was no way we could grab everything in one night, but with Mary's help and Damien turning a purposeful blind eye to us, we had everyone's belongings and a good bit of furniture moved over. We had to convert a few of the lower rooms to bedrooms, and it was a small bit of a squeeze, but it would work for now.

"Not a bad spot here at all." Darren winked, tossing me a duffel bag that was heavier than it looked. "You do know alpha status doesn't get you out of lifting? Put that super strength to some use."

I laughed, dropping the bag in the hall by the front door. "It's pretty nice, if I say so myself. Remind me why I put you in charge of the move?"

"Because you love me, really," he joked, wearing his signature lopsided grin. "Besides, you can't get everyone here a job and roll out your grand plans without plenty of help."

I couldn't argue with that. Darren had been amazing. I couldn't have formed the pack without him. The plan was to settle in the Kildare house for a few months and slowly work on getting everyone their own houses, all staying close, but I wanted the pack to properly integrate with society. Larissa wasn't too pleased, but she agreed we were to be given a good chunk of the law firm's money, which Damien was not happy with either. Something told me the royals weren't totally aware of her meddling and that she wanted to keep me quiet. I was in no position to take her on, and I didn't want any more bloodshed. That was a battle for another day.

We had almost enough to fund a house deposit for each pack member or family to get us started. With normal jobs, each family could pay their mortgage and lead a quiet life. That's what we were about, living a happy life alongside humans.

I sighed, rubbing my face with my palm. "I hate leaving her behind."

"I know, but she made that choice, and no one can change Mary's mind once it's made up."

"I wish I could."

Darren shrugged, leaning against the door frame. "She wanted to keep an eye on Damien. We know he's going to be up to something shady with those witches. That pack was her father's legacy, so I can understand why she couldn't walk away."

"I guess," I muttered, unable to shake the sense of regret.

"You have your own pack to worry about now," Darren continued, giving me a hefty clap on the back. "Your family needs you, so keep your head in the now. We've a busy few months ahead."

He was right. I was working shifts at the hospital, living the life I had always wanted, but being an alpha and a dad on top of that, I was triple jobbing. If it hadn't been for Helena, I'd have fallen apart.

She walked back over, Luke settled in her arms and playing with her hair.

"I see the unpacking is going well," she teased, a small smile playing on her lips as she nudged a black bag with her foot.

"I don't see you helping!" Darren laughed as he dumped yet another bag in the hall and dragged me back out to the car to give him a hand with the rest.

Helena watched from the doorway, Luke balanced on her hip. *My family.*

I dropped a bag outside the door and caught her expression soften.

"What's wrong?" I asked, leaning in to give her a peck on the cheek. "You're not feeling sick, are you?"

She shook her head, those emerald eyes filled with emotion. "Nope, not today, so far."

I studied her face a moment longer.

"I just never thought this would be possible. I never thought I'd have this...." She trailed off, emotion choking her words.

"Me neither."

As if on cue, Luke planted a kiss on her cheek and then proceeded to blow a raspberry which made both of us laugh.

I wrapped an arm around her waist and looked around at our garden, our new neighbourhood and couldn't resist a smile as she placed a hand on the small bump on her stomach. "I never imagined this either, but I'm so glad I came back here and found you."

"And your pack," she reminded me with a wry smile.

"And my pack." The words still felt weird on my tongue. I wondered when it would ever feel normal.

The sky a bright blue with splashes of pink along the horizon where dawn was giving way. Cloudless, a rarity in Ireland, and to the west, the faint outline of the moon was visible in its crescent phase. Luke broke the moment by squealing when he noticed a plane leaving a white trail in its wake.

"I finally know the name." I placed one arm around Helena's shoulder, pointing out the setting moon to my son. "See that? We're the Crescent Pack, because while the moon controls our change, we are not only our wolf side. Power isn't the magic that allows us to shift. True power comes from within."

As if on cue to ruin a moving moment, Darren rounded the corner with a pink suitcase in toe dragging along the gravel.

He stuck out his tongue at us, pretending to retch. "Gross. If you're done being all lovey-dovey, there's a car full of *your* stuff that needs unpacking."

I rolled my eyes and Helena laughed, ushering me towards his beloved Maria.

"You know, just because I'm your beta doesn't mea—"

I cut Darren off, arching an eyebrow. "Since when did I give you a title?"

His phone buzzed and his grin only widened at the sight of the caller ID flashing on the screen, dumping the suitcase in the hallway before pressing the phone to his ear.

"Shane? Is everything okay?" He asked, his brow furrowing as concern washed over his features.

Once the pack formed, we had put plans in place to get them home as soon as it was safe for them all to travel. What with it being so close to the birth, Gráinne couldn't stomach the boat ride.

I could only make out snippets due to the buzzing on the line, but any worry was quickly replaced by the biggest smile lighting up my best friend's face. The corners of his eyes creased and he reached out to squeeze Helena's shoulder, easing her look of confusion.

"It's a girl," he announced, his words bursting with joy. "I have a baby niece!"

Helena squealed, throwing her arms around Darren in celebration. My friend reached out, pulling me into their giant hug with Luke at the centre, his pink cheeks dimpling as he smiled. The little guy had no idea what was happening, yet he smiled simply at the show of happiness. I would walk through the fiery pits of hell ten times over make sure my son knew happiness and love.

Helena was bouncing on her tiptoes with excitement, almost giving me a black eye in the process as she passed me Luke and then proceeded to try grapple the phone off Darren.

"The first Crescent baby," I murmured, kissing the top of Luke's head as I set him down.

I brushed my fingertips over the ring-box in the pocket of my slacks, the corners of my lips kicking up as I watched my son race after Helena as she screamed with laughter wrestling with Darren. Our future and that of the Crescent pack was bright.

AUTHOR NOTE

Thank you so much for reading Lone Wolf! This book was written during the pandemic just before my life was turned upside-down. In some ways, it feels like a different person wrote this book because I've changed so much, but as always, art imitates life in the most peculiar ways.

It was nice to ask family about life in Dublin in the 90's because I as only a baby then. Being able to incorporate stories like how girls used to get the bus into the city and meet their date beneath the Clery's clock or Bewley's café which has been around for one hundred years was pretty cool.

Tom will hold a special place in my heart because he wasn't afraid to fight for what he believed in. Even if it meant losing loved ones, or going against blood, he used his voice and fought for those who needed someone to stand up for them. He's a reluctant hero, often viewing himself as an anti-hero. And I think a lot of us breaking generational trauma can relate to him.

I'm an indie author juggling writing with a full-time job. So, if you could spare two minutes to post a review it would mean the world to me.

Hearing from readers is one of my favourite things. Come hang out with me to talk anything books!

Newsletter: www.ciaradelahunt.com/newsletter
PNR Book Club: www.discord.com/invite/dWCFbYGZFz
Reader Group: Ciara's Book Coven

ACKNOWLEDGMENTS

Tom's story came to me so easily. Like Luke, his character will always have a special place in my heart. I think he stands for the kind of parent so many of us wish we had.

Writing isn't easy and I would have never made it this far without an army of wonderful people behind me. To every person in my life who encouraged me to take a chance on this, thank you. *Lone Wolf* almost stayed a newsletter prequel, and it deserves so much more than that. It deserves a full book and to sit pretty on bookshelves alongside the rest of the *Hybrid Wolf Series*.

Thank you to every reader who signed up to read *Lone Wolf* back when it was *Killer Instinct*. To the OGs on Instagram who have followed be on this journey, especially those who beta read my books, thank you for helping me make this dream a reality. Special thanks to Jodi and Fran for being amazing, inspirational women and cheerleading me from the start. Kara, thank you for working your magic on my books.

To my friends and family for supporting me on this journey, I am so lucky to have you. Thank you, mam, for passing on your love of books. And for all the info from the nineties that I was too young to remember. It's been a bit of a rollercoaster, but what good adventure isn't?

Finally, thank you to my partner for putting up with my craziness. From listening to my ideas, the plot twists I blurt out at random whether it's during the day or the middle of the night, to reminding me to find balance and look after myself.

You always make me feel like I can take on the world. You've supported me every step of the way, and I'm so incredibly grateful to share the journey with you.

To you, the reader, thank you for taking a chance on this chaotic Irish girl with a dream.

About the Author

Ciara writes paranormal romance with dark twists, spice, and a heavy dose of sarcasm. Her books feature strong women, morally grey love interests, suspense, and found family. She lives in the Irish countryside with her boyfriend and their two cats. When she doesn't have her head stuck in a book, you will find Ciara walking in the parklands nearby, in the gym, passed out on her yoga mat, or screaming at a rugby match.

A book-dragon from birth, her love of reading bled into writing when she was a teenager, and the rest is history. Ciara can't write without music and loves nothing more than to be curled up with her laptop and a mocha in her favourite coffee shop, writing to her heart's content.

amazon.com/author/ciaradelahunt

tiktok.com/@ciaradelahuntbooks

instagram.com/ciaradelahunt

facebook.com/authorciaradelahunt

threads.net/@ciaradelahunt

bsky.app/profile/ciaradelahunt.bsky.social

bookbub.com/authors/ciara-delahunt

goodreads.com/ciaradelahunt